IOWA WEIRD VOL. I

HAYSEED PRESS LLC

HAYSEED PRESS

CONTENTS

Introduction 5

1. The Weeping Woman of the Cedar 9
   By Lauren Riensche

2. Coal Eaters: The Van Meter Visitors 16
   By Aaron Narigon

3. Young Love in a Storm 24
   By Michael Kaufman

4. Dust-Up 34
   By Marc Dickinson

5. A.I.owa 44
   By Anton Jones

6. The Quiet Room 58
   By Kara Thorstenson

7. Lake Red Rock 66
   By Chad Douglas

8. The Detasseling 87
   By Cole Thorna

9. No Toe   106
    By Edward Narigon

10. Guests in the Parlor   114
    By Jenny Fee

11. Dark Matter   126
    By Kevin Klingman

12. Demons from Ahigh   136
    By Nick Narigon

13. Battle for Marengo   159
    By Alexander C. Bailey

14. Brood Parasite   187
    By Wes Smith

15. Venganza's Curse   203
    By Peter Boylan

16. Don't Touch Jenny's Things   218
    By Dace Carlisle

History & Hauntings of Downtown CF

Sign up to stay informed

linktr.ee/cfghosttour

INTRODUCTION

Growing up in Iowa, my favorite campfire ghost story was *The Golden Arm*. My father, Edward Narigon, told the best version on Indian Guide campouts way back in the '80s when I was just a kindergartener. He continued telling the story at every Cub Scout and Boy Scout campout causing teenage boys to choke on their S'mores.

The key to the story is to get quieter and eerier as the tale nears its conclusion and then shout, "I've got it!" while grabbing one of the unsuspecting Scouts. I developed my own version of *The Golden Arm* when I became a Scout leader, changing the characters and setting depending on the location of the campout.

Then last summer while camping at Backbone State Park in Iowa I was able to share *The Golden Arm* with my own sons. They haven't slept since.

The idea to produce *Iowa Weird Vol. 1* came last year shortly after the launch of Hayseed Press. I was still living in Singapore and I came across Russell Lee's collection, *True Singapore Ghost Stories*. For 25 years Lee collected true ghost stories from readers in Singapore and Malaysia, printing a new anthology every year.

Some stories were classic legends simply relocated to Singapore, such as the story of the guy who picked up a girl on the side of the road and gave her his jacket only to return to her house the next day to retrieve the jacket and find it lying atop her gravestone, or the school girl who died of cancer and returned in ghostly form to hand in her homework.

There were also stories based on Malay mythology, such as stories about *pontianaks* (the dark spirits of women who died in childbirth) or of women who used *susoks* (mystical needles that when inserted deep in the scalp keep a woman young and beautiful forever).

We have these same stories in Iowa. Not necessarily women with magical needles stuck in their skulls, but we do have ghost stories. A sheriff's deputy once told me he moved into a country farmhouse specifically because it was haunted. He said a ghostly woman in an old cotton dress regularly walked up the stairs and disappeared as soon as she reached the second floor.

I had my own experience in New Mexico when late one night I heard the footsteps of the headless miner's daughter walking across a meadow.

So I reached out to the Hayseed Press community requesting you all send in your best true Iowa ghost stories. I received a lot of enthusiasm but no material. Thankfully one of our devoted newsletter subscribers put us in touch with Lauren Riensche, founder of Cedar Falls Ghost Tour.

Lauren's work with Cedar Falls Ghost Tour was inspiring, but also highlighted how daunting it can be to extract personal stories from Iowans. Lauren literally had to go door-to-door in downtown Cedar Falls asking business owners if they had ghost stories to share. Based in Singapore, that tactic was going to be difficult for me.

So I changed tactics. Rather than share true ghost stories, we broadened the subject matter of our short story collection. Thus *Iowa Weird Vol. 1* was born. We reached out to all of our writer friends and asked them to write a spooky, creepy, or out-of-this-world short story. It could be based on a true story or created totally from imagination.

The only instruction was that the story had to be based in Iowa. They did not disappoint. (Though our dear friend Peter Boylan out in Honolulu—the most diehard Hawkeye fan you will meet—didn't quite follow the one rule. C'est la vie—he submitted a wonderfully weird story nonetheless.)

Lauren turned in a true ghost story from Cedar Falls that has me anxious to explore the north shore of the Cedar River the next time I return home. Anton Jones, MFA (Iowa Playwrights' Workshop) and two-time Jerome Many Voices Fellow, delivered us a juxtaposition of what happens when rural Iowa and ChatGTP cross paths (and unfortunately copyright laws prevented us from naming the real culprit—Iowa's most famous and delicious loose meat sandwich).

We have an existential battle with Iowa's weather written by award-winning short story writer Marc Dickinson as well as a deep dive into the dark underbelly of libraries from Kara Thorstenson, who happens to be a librarian. Plus this issue features an intensive investigation into Iowa's own mythical creature as written by Hayseed Press co-founder, and my brother, Aaron Narigon.

Finally, I would be remiss if I didn't mention, and give a full-hearted thank you to Jackson Moore of CHARM Co-op for designing the front cover of *Iowa Weird Vol. 1*. Thanks for allowing us to note you to death, and for delivering a cover that encapsulates the ethos of the mythos contained within.

Sit back, relax, and get weird.

—Nick Narigon
Co-founder Hayseed Press
hayseed@hayseedpress.com

1

THE WEEPING WOMAN OF THE CEDAR

By Lauren Riensche

The Cedar River — The Lifeblood of Cedar Falls

The Cedar River is the lodestone of Cedar Falls. Since the town's inception, the Cedar River has supplied the water needed for drinking, cooking, cleaning, bathing, and, most notably, powered the town's earliest mills. Timbered banks provided the raw material for early buildings; game in the riparian woods fed and clothed an expanding number of households. The town's first infrastructure was not street nor rail but current.

William Sturgis saw the river's potential. In 1845, he claimed land and built a cabin near the shore, and soon after, began construction on a dam. After two years, progress on the dam had been slower than expected; and so when the Overman family came to the area and offered to purchase Sturgis' claim, William jumped at the chance.

The Overmans began by imposing a sharper order on the flow of the river. In the 1850s, they cut the Mills Race—a narrow, shallow offshoot of the river engineered to accelerate water for mill wheels. For more than a century, that channel translated the Cedar River's motion into municipal growth. Although the Mills Race was eventually filled in in 1971, its legacy has lasted into the modern day.

Despite the tremendous value the river brought the Cedar Falls community, the river was also undoubtedly dangerous. Warmer months brought fast undercurrents and swiftly flowing rapids; colder months saw ice floes and falls into the frozen water. Accidents, rescues, and deaths prevailed, no matter the season. The town quickly learned a hard-and-fast rule: the river gives, and the river also takes.

Tragedy in Summer 1891

In July 1891, sixteen-year-old Mary Thompson, and her sister Bertha, eighteen, joined friends for a jaunt along the Cedar River north of town. Strolling along the sandy banks was a common activity, and on hot days, so was wading into the water to help combat the pressing heat. Families and groups pitched canvas tents under trees, cooked over small fires, and sought relief from high temperatures.

That fateful summer day, Mary, Bertha, and their friends returned to visit a spot in the river they were familiar with. They favored this location because they knew the bank there to have a gradual slope, allowing them to wade further into the river without it becoming too deep.

However, recent floods earlier that spring had dramatically changed that slope. Floodwater had shifted away sand and mud, resulting in a steep drop-off where the bottom had previously extended at a gentle grade. This change was invisible from the shore.

Hand in hand, the sisters entered the river. A friend paralleled them in a small boat, chatting with the sisters as they progressed. They advanced into the water as they had for many years, trusting the bank they believed they knew.

Suddenly, both sisters tumbled off the edge of the underwater drop-off. Mary and Bertha's hands were ripped apart, and laden down by layers of clothing, they both slipped under the surface.

Incredibly, Bertha managed to scramble her way back to the surface of the water, near enough to her friend's boat to cling onto the side and take stock of her surroundings. Within seconds, she noticed that Mary had not yet reappeared. And so, without a second thought, she released her hold on the boat and dove beneath the surface. That was the last time either sister was seen alive.

For hours, friends, family, and neighbors walked the banks of the river, probing near drift lines and scrutinizing every eddy for the smallest sign of the girls. The river often returned what it took, but on its own schedule—and this case was no different.

The sisters' bodies washed up on shore that evening, just a few miles downstream. Their bodies were found, recovered, and brought back to their parents' home. As unimaginably terrible as this ordeal was for the Thompson family, it was unfortunately not the end of tragedy for them.

Not long after Mary and Bertha's deaths, their toddler brother died by horse kick. Their surviving brother later married but eventually committed his wife to the Mental Health Institute in Independence, Iowa. These and other subsequent tragedies for the family were not caused by the river, necessarily, but residents folded them into the narrative of the

Thompsons, reading the 1891 drowning as the first in a series of blows for the household.

The Weeping Woman

Reports of an apparition of a young woman along the banks of the Cedar River began shortly after the sisters' deaths. And, the story is all the more compelling for its consistency over the past century.

It goes like this. Someone will be spending time along the north bank of the Cedar River, near the shore where the drowning took place. There are many trails and tranquil areas in the vicinity used by hikers, bicyclists, and anglers. One of these visitors will spot a solitary woman walking the bank, most often at dusk, and they all describe her similarly—she's wearing a long, dark brown dress, with her light brown hair up in a Gibson girl style, and frequently, she is described as weeping quietly into her hands as she paces the shore.

Many visitors find themselves, understandably, concerned to see a young woman crying by herself at this spot in the river. They begin approaching her, but when they get within one hundred feet, she walks rapidly away and eventually disappears. Some say she vanishes around a bend, behind a tree, or into thin air. Regardless, no one has ever gotten close enough to reach out or see her face.

The dress, hairstyle, and location along the river associated with this apparition fit the story well. While the spirit may be that of either sister, most speculate that the young woman is Bertha Thompson, distraught and eternally continuing her search for Mary.

An Enduring Legacy

Cedar Falls owes its existence to the Cedar River, and it has paid the price of that debt many times over. While the 1891 loss of Mary and Bertha Thompson is one of the town's most poignant reminders of that exchange, hundreds have met their end in the burgeoning waters of the Cedar.

The town has grown and changed immensely over the years—the Mills Race was built and then filled, streets were platted and then paved, businesses came and went. And through it all, the river has persisted, as has the story of the Thompson sisters, pointing us toward a bend and a bank where still today residents say a solitary figure sometimes walks and weeps.

***

About the Author

Lauren Riensche is a Cedar Valley local and haunted history buff. Lauren has always been fascinated by how spooky stories find themselves embedded in a community's lore and history, and she has taken dozens of ghost tours in cities around the world. Now, she shares her passion for history and the supernatural with tourgoers via the Cedar Falls Ghost Tour. Founded by Lauren in 2021, the Cedar Falls Ghost Tour has not only sold out every year, but has also brought over 3000 tourists from more than 60 communities across the country to Cedar Falls.

The success of the tour has given Lauren the opportunity to donate over $10,000 in proceeds to local non-profits and partner with more than 40 area businesses to host private tours, purchase goods and services, offer visibility and recruitment opportunities, and provide unique tourism experiences. The tour has been featured in dozens of publications, bringing Cedar Falls to the attention of over 1M+ viewers, listeners, and readers. Beyond the tour, Lauren works in agricultural marketing, is active in volunteering for Community Main Street in Cedar Falls and for her alma mater, the University of Chicago, and enjoys taking on projects in her mid-century home with her high school sweetheart husband, Luke.

2

COAL EATERS: THE VAN METER VISITORS

BY AARON NARIGON

Found in a decomposing letter inside a tin box buried next to a large boulder in a field in Central Iowa, 2023:

I am writing this now because I feel my story needs told, and I fear something is catching up to me. My name is [indecipherable] and I came to Iowa from places East as a vagrant fifteen year old hoping to find easy work, but after no luck in Des Moines ended up near the coal mines west of there. I'd just set foot in Van Meter fall of 1903, where word east was they had their hands full. And I wasn't the only one drifting in on the freight lines under similar impressions.

Turns out Iowa coal is some of the stinkiest shit you will ever come across, too much sulfur. Can't get the rotten egg smell out of your nose once it's burned in there. And the seams were way too thin for big teams, already well-worked by old English and Welshmen who hired immigrants to work for pennies. The big haul was only because they kept pushing deeper. I was starving and about to make my case to Platt the Mine Director himself for any job they had so long as I could get some food for supper. Before I could, the mayor shows up grim and embarrassed and calls him before the City Elders. I wasn't invited, but I had nothing so I went with and pretended to belong.

It was a commotion in the town hall. Seemed like everyone was there, women and children scared and stricken, men covering up their scared acting busy. A few smirked. They all shouted at Platt at once til someone got them calmed down to speak one by one.

The first to go was a businessman, well-spoken. Five days before at the end of September he'd worked late and at 1 am was making his way home down Main. A sudden glow started up ahead of him, like a street light burning a hole in the ground. He saw smoke curling up from the edges. Thinking it vandals, he shouted up a challenge. The light swung to him, burning for an instant and even from that distance blinding him. When his vision returned the building was still. He heard a creak of metal, and looked up to see something dark glide across the street and land on another building. Still thinking vandals, he challenged again, and this time it soared directly above him. He ran then, not turning for a block. When he did, he saw whatever it was leap and glide to the next closest pole. He took off and didn't look again until he was home with the door locked and barred. The next day he told others and they went up to the roof of the buildings. Found nothing. In the Town Hall, arguments started everywhere.

Dr. Alcott kept trying to speak and once everyone shushed he was next to go. Four nights earlier just after midnight he'd been trying to sleep on a back cot in his office, but the story going around town kept him up. Of a sudden a burning light shot through the room, and he floundered out of bed and into his boots. He also grabbed his revolver and headed out the back door.

Dr. Alcott, he took a minute to tell the next bit, and only after others prodded him on. He told how the thing on the wall was all huge leathery wings that spread across the building, long curved talons ending each and clasping the bricks. It was climbing up next to the opening, searching, its long beaked head sporting a horn that pointed forward, from which the light poured as it scanned through the window. Its body hung down, black, skinny, and dreadful. Overcome, the doctor fired, sure he had hit the beast. It shrieked and found his gaze, which became a blinding flash of pain in his eyes and face. The last thing he saw was its leap off the building, directly towards him. The doctor shot his remaining rounds as he fell on his back, unable to see and sure of a gruesome death. His eyes cleared several moments later and he was able to witness it flying off into the distance. The next day they found casings, some bullets, but no blood or gore or other leavings of a wounded being. Dr. Alcott hadn't slept since that night, and he shook as he told his story.

Next the bank teller spoke up. A young man, he rushed through how he'd been sleeping at the bank with a shotgun due to all the talk. The very next night he was awoken after 1 am by a horrid gurgling sound outside the window. Terrified, he approached the opening when he was pinned by the intense burning light. The light moved through the room in a slow steady motion. When the light swung off him, the teller described what he could then see. Directly behind the window stared an enlarged human-like face, beaked and the beak lined with teeth. And coal black eyes which met his. The gurgling got louder and as the awful light pinned him again he fired the shotgun right at the demonic face at near point blank range. The light disappeared, then was upon him again, blinding and burning his eyes and face. He screamed in terror and fell and when he could see again the monster was gone. The morning light showed multiple footprints with three clawed toes, lightly indented and scattered outside the window. But no sign that the creature bled or even hurt from the shotgun blast.

Platt started a smarmy placation then, but was shouted down with the chant of hear us out! He held up his hands, and the Hardware store owner stepped forward. He looked like a big whig in town and the hall quieted immediately. His story was from only the night previous, he also hadn't slept. After midnight he'd heard awful sounds outside his building, and went out to investigate with his gun. Atop the telephone post beside his building perched a creature like a gargoyle, regarding him. Another shopkeeper heard the commotion as well and stepped out, then let out a shout. The monster reared up on its perch, snapping its wings wide. The most foul smell he had ever known slammed into the hardware store owner and he became delirious. He was sick and had to stay there, hands on knees heaving for a long time before the air cleared enough. He found the other shopkeeper lying there unconscious in his own sick. He shook the shopkeeper awake, then they caught sight of the horror soaring towards the abandoned mine on the edge of town. They decided something ought to be done.

In the Town Hall he demanded such and the mayor looked at Platt meaningfully. Platt at first tried to joke that his job description didn't include dealing with make believe monsters. No one laughed. His smile fell, he sighed, muttered bloody fucking hell, and admitted that some of his older foremen had been warning him they'd dug too deep into the vein. Something about upsetting the Coblynau. He didn't believe in such nonsense, but over the past week he'd been getting reports from miners near the abandoned shaft of mysterious sounds and smells where there should be none. He couldn't pay any of them enough to investigate further.

Seeing my opportunity, I jumped up to volunteer. So did many others, enough men with their own weapons that I quickly got fired before I even had the job. As the posse formed up, I was appealing to Platt, trying to scrape any opportunity out of this madness. He ignored me and I only stopped when one of the posse grabbed my arm and took me aside. He'd actually paid Platt to join up, being an outsider, and he was a mousy, dirty man, stained with seemingly years of coal and grime. He held up a quarter dollar and that got my full attention, said it was mine if I'd help him carry his ruck. I grabbed that quarter and he tossed me his rucksack and we headed out into the night.

The posse split up into shifts and then teams and we stationed up just before it got dark, spread out and hidden in locations that gave a view to and from the entrance of the mine. It seemed we could hardly get settled, and before we could react two winged figures emerged from the entrance and flew off. The guy partnered with us ran to town to let everyone else know. The man who hired me kept muttering in excitement, getting agitated then calming over and again. He asked me if I had seen the Coal Eaters before, the monster. I told him I was new in town, from out east and didn't know anything. He was from West Virginia, said he'd been a coal miner until crawling into a Coal Eater deep in a clandestine shaft. He'd become a researcher then, a gatherer of lore, stories, and evidence of them ever since. Old miners tales to some, but West Virginia was full of them. Coblynau. Bucca Dhu. Caoránach. They consumed the coal from the underneath while we mined it from atop. Sometimes we'd mine too deep and let the Coal Eaters out. Sometimes that was ok. Often it was not.

He took out a shard of something and then let me hold it so I could see it close. It looked like a large snake scale, long and wide as my thumb and feather light, shining black. I held it by the edges at first until they cut into my fingers and I realized it was made of a tough, razor thin metal. A Coal Eater scale, he said as he took it back and stowed it in his pocket. He thought the smell, the horn, the scales, came from those impurities all coal held to varying degrees, and which they consumed with the coal.

He wanted to catch one. To show the world. To become rich. He thought this was his chance. He'd read the *Charleston News & Courier* page ten newspaper report and rushed to the Midwest on the first train. He had a stout fishing net and a camera ready for when the Coal Eaters returned. If I helped he would be able to reward me more handsomely than I could ever imagine.

The full posse returned hours later, weary but edgy and armed with rifles, shotguns, pistols, knives, dynamite. There was an immediate argument with my benefactor, who wanted the weapons put away. They were no use, he said. He tried to convince them to let him attempt a capture, and when that didn't work he paid them to. They set up in a loose ring around the mine entrance, hidden in bush and fen. I followed West Virginia (for I never learned his name) with my side of the net. We found a Cypress ten feet from the entrance to hole down behind. Then we waited.

An hour before dawn it was so still we heard them calling and winging in and had a second to prepare. We pulled up the net as they landed, and WV led us forward. I was trying to stay low, move forward, hold the net, and see what I was moving towards. There were two of them, one twice the size of the other, both long and sleek and shining with what light reflected off their scaled hide in ripples as they moved. I could see how WV could become enchanted, they were beautiful and awful and overwhelming. They had landed on their back legs, standing like a man for a moment before curling their wings and dropping to all fours. That was when WV lunged, and I meant to follow suit.

But the net must have caught up my foot while I was gawking at the Coal Eaters, and when WV lunged I went down hard on my shoulder. I heard him swear, realized he couldn't throw the net with my weight on it, then heard he and the Coal Eaters all scream at the same time. The night lit up, bright and fiery, and shrieks like ripping metal met the mortal shrieks of a human in heart-wrenching pain. Then someone shot. Then everyone shot and for a while all I could hear and sense was blast after blast of every weapon being discharged over and over in my general area. I spied the large Coal Eater, wings furled around the smaller one, its wing membranes bouncing and rebounding in circular waves, round after round after round.

There was a cessation of the gunfire when the Coal Eaters both spread their wings wide and the smell, worse than a baby shitting out rotten eggs, flooded the place. I was retching. The posse was retching. Between heaves I watched the Coal Eaters descend into the mine.

Thirty minutes later the posse had procured shovels and were backfilling the mine entrance with a will. Just inside the entrance was too much dynamite and the bullet riddled body of my dear dead benefactor. Much of his face had been burned away and disfigured, his eyes fried crispy, his ruined mouth agape.

The posse promised me food after the job was done, but they spoke a little too loudly while debating whether or not what had just happened was murder or manslaughter or just an accident. Whether to pin the death upon me or just add me to the pile. I was only a vagabond outsider after all. I was miles away when they blew the mine entrance, but my borrowed horse still almost threw me and it took miles more to get it back under control.

I went north, avoiding the settlements, releasing the horse and ending up along the Des Moines River, fishing and trapping and hiding to stay alive. They sent someone after me. So I keep moving, and they keep catching up. And now it's getting colder and I am not sure what is next. Not sure I care anymore. So I wrote this, and now hide this, so someone can find it someday and know what really happened.

God Bless the man whose death came from my tragic error. And God Damn those monsters in Van Meter.

***

About the Author

Hayseed Press co-founder Aaron Narigon holds a Master of Arts in English Language and Literature from University of Northern Iowa. He is a Professor of English and has taught at Hawkeye Community College since 2002. Currently Aaron coordinates Middlemoot, the Midwest's premier biennial Tolkien conference, and is the co-editor of UKL, the only scholarly journal dedicated to the work of Ursula K. LeGuin.

3

YOUNG LOVE IN A STORM

BY MICHAEL KAUFMAN

The night was hot, and lightning streaked through the sky like gold veins on black emptiness as the thunder followed in booms and rattles. We were in my Chevy pickup with the windows cracked blending us and the bugs and the country in one long humid breath. The flashes of lightning showed our eyes and sweaty faces. The great flashes showed the rickety old barn we were parked beside and the tall, late summer corn standing all around blocking our pleasures from the world. I could feel the weather as much as I could feel her like we were already thousands of miles apart and together only in memories. She was different in that storm. Her hair and cross necklace dangled in front of and against my face. I didn't know if she was mindfully there with me or thinking of something divine which she truly believed in, but it didn't matter. Deep down I think we both knew it was our farewell. It's not so much that you don't know something at the time, you just don't believe it yet. The present was all that existed and all that ever would.

She sat against me in the back seat breathing heavily, both catching our breath. The rain started in at sprinkle and picked up, hearing it against the roof, to a heavy downpour. We both reached forward around seats and rolled the windows up.

"That was something," she said.

"Maybe the best ever," I said.

I could see her smile in a flash of lightning.

"We were supposed to be talking about things," she said.

"We were."

"Hardly."

"You told me to pull over," I said.

"I wanted to see what it was like down this driveway."

"Creepy... kind of," I said. "That's why I locked the doors."

"It's a good spot for fooling around," she said.

"It is that," I said. "Someone lived here once. Someone with dreams and ambitions."

"And love," she said. "Not everyone wants what they don't have."

"I don't mean to," I said.

"Then don't join the Navy. It's that simple."

"It's not," I said.

"You haven't committed. You could still back out."

"Then what would that make me?"

"Settled. In love. Like you say you are."

"I do love you," I said.

"Actions are louder than words aren't they."

We sat there a moment in silence, naked, close, but seeming as far apart as us and the people who once lived on that farmstead. I found my underwear and put it on.

"So, you got what you wanted and now that's it," she said.

"It's hot in here. We better get going anyways. Your parents will be wondering where we are."

"Why can't you be honest?" she said.

"I am. I told you. I've told you before. I have to do what I'm doing. I can't stay here and get old doing nothing but farming or working some bullshit nine to five job like I'm dead already."

She began to cry. I tried to hold her, but she pushed me away and looked out the window. I sat there listening to her sniffles and the thunder. What could I do, I wondered. Was I wrong? Maybe I drug it on too long. We were nearly done before but were held on because we tried crawling away instead of walking. I knew I was going and nothing was changing that. She was still in school, and I was out and leaving. I remembered feeling jealous. Jealous of what would happen after. Someone else would be loving her. Perhaps that held me up. Jealousy was there alright, in all its gnashing and clawing ways. Maybe I was wrong, I thought. How do I know what I want. If she is right, then I should hang on and just be. What was I chasing? The sudden rush of losing something dear to me came on where it makes all your decisions to that moment seem foolish and makes you question it all and second guess your ideals and beliefs and makes you want to crawl back admitting mistake.

"What was that?" I thought I heard her say.

"What?"

"What was that?"

"I didn't see anything," I said.

"There was someone by those weeds," she said hysterically. "Beside the barn."

"I can't see anything."

"I swear I saw kids," she said.

Lightning lit the whole sky and the ghoulish barn and the waving corn. I scanned the weeds which were whipping around in the wind. I saw nothing.

"There!" she jumped and pointed forward to the front of the pickup.

I looked and saw nothing but the windshield and the darkness beyond.

"Get us out of here!" she said.

I climbed over the middle console hurriedly and stumbling wondering if she was tricking or if it was real.

"Hurry!" she said. She climbed into the passenger seat still naked.

As I grabbed the wheel with one hand and the key with the other, she let out a goose bumped, adrenaline scream. I looked to see the points of a pitchfork against the passenger window then sliding down in a drawn-out screech. The forks disappeared and slowly appeared the head of an old man, bone faced and whiskered, looking through the two of us. He looked like me if I were old. My hands were gripped to the wheel and the keys.

"Start the truck!" she screamed.

I turned the key, and the 350 Chevy came to life with thunder of its own. I turned the lights on, shifted to reverse, and hit the gas with my right foot shaken and heavy. Immediately I knew there was a flat tire making the wheel difficult to turn as we wobbled backwards. The storm seemed louder now and the flashes brighter bringing the whole abandoned farm to life. I saw nothing in the mirrors but black and rain and dim, red, reverse lights. I turned to look back and it was the same.

"I can't see shit!" I said.

"He's coming!" she said. "Keep going!"

I had my foot down, turned around looking for driveway or road. We were moving backwards was all I knew. I felt the wheel jerk, corrected it, then was whiplashed against the seat as we crashed into something. I looked out my window and saw, with lightning, we were half in the weeds and had hit something covered by time and overgrowth. I jammed the shifter into drive and matted the gas. The power hit the wheels but only spun them. I felt for the four-wheel-drive shifter, the dash and floor lights beaming, shoved it into four-wheel-drive and gave it another try. The tail end drifted to the side, scratching against whatever it was, but made no progress.

"He's coming!" she said.

I looked up into the glow of the headlights and saw the old man, pitchfork in hand, coming toward us, emotionless, through the rain. Two kids in tattered clothes and bare feet ran left to right behind him disappearing out of view. I sat still for a moment feeling as though I could not move.

"What are you doing?" she said.

"We're stuck," I said.

"Do something."

I opened the center console and felt for my pistol, pulling it from its holster, and racking a round from the inserted magazine, then pushing the safety off. I looked back up and saw no one.

"Where did he go?" I said.

"I don't know," she said. She began reciting the Lord's prayer.

I scanned the scene trying to think.

"I've got no service on my phone," she said.

"Wait here," I said slipping on my shoes but still in my underwear.

"No!" she cried. "Don't get out."

"We're stuck. We're going to have to run."

"Don't leave me."

"I've got to make sure we're clear to run."

"Just stay here."

"Lock the doors as soon as I'm out," I said.

I shut the pickup off and killed the lights. The rain went on. The wind pressed. Lightning flashed. We both jumped at the crack of thunder. Shakey and heart racing I opened the door feeling the rain immediately. Squeeze the trigger, I thought. Steady. Be steady. Head on a swivel.

"Don't," I heard her say as I slammed the door, both hands on the pistol in the ready position.

The wind hit me as the weeds soaked my legs and shoes instantly, and the rain, my hair and shoulders. Everything was wet, taking the heat away. I stepped through the weeds piling them over. I felt the taillight with my left hand keeping the pistol up with my right. With my foot I felt the obstacle blocking the pickup which I assumed was an old field cultivator. I saw no one in the flashes. Boom went the thunder, and I jumped. I wiped rain from my face. More flashes in the distance over the hills and I could see the ditch and road. Another flash and I saw several figures moving quickly by two tall, oak trees that once shaded a yard. I raised my pistol and fired a few shots where I thought they might be in the darkness.

I felt a sharp pain in my back near my shoulder, slamming me into the fender, letting out a wail, dropping my pistol, falling to my knees, then feeling whatever it was being pulled back out. I fell to my side, reaching and feeling for my pistol, finding it, coming around wielding it, seeing the forks pass in front of my face as I fired several shots. My ears were ringing. I smelled gunpowder and worms. The pitchfork was gone but out of the darkness it stabbed into my thigh, through it, and into the ground beneath. I jolted and groaned. In another flash I saw the old man laying as I was, wounded. I could see the white of his eyes, his emptiness there at my feet. The pitchfork handle stuck straight up out my leg. The two of us were seeing the last of the other. I shot him in the head, whiplashing him before he fell, lifeless.

What I was unaware of in my own struggle was what had happened with the figures crossing the ghostly yard. They were young men moving like coyotes after what was left of us. I had not heard the passenger window being shattered or the screams as she tried to fight them off before being yanked from the pickup. They were courting her the way demons would.

I lay back on the wet ground, adrenaline pumping. I was shaking, looking up at the stormy night, blinking in the rain, smelling blood now. Her screams registered. I sat up and grabbed the pitchfork handle with both hands. I felt the pain shoot through my leg to my neck like a shock. I let go immediately. Gut wrenching screams. Pull it out! I thought. I grabbed the handle once more and yanked it out feeling my leg release from the ground then fell back dropping the pitchfork to my side.

I grabbed the pistol then turned over to crawl beneath the pickup through weeds leaving blood behind in the grass not feeling the pain anymore. I crawled through wetness hearing shrieks getting further away. On the other side of the pickup, I crawled out pistol ready to fire. I saw nothing until lightning crashed like distant artillery as though we were a small skirmish in something much larger that we never understood. She was looking at me with outstretched arms digging at the ground being dragged away by her bare legs. She called to me like a lover fading into the past. I shot at those dragging her. One fell but others took his place like flag bearers. Some turned back to face me. I heard the unmistakable sound of a maddening dog.

Before I knew it the hound was a blur in my peripherals and then a sharp pain in my arm I had put out as defense. Its momentum knocked me over as its teeth sank into my flesh as I struggled to fight it off. I was on my back with the dog atop me clawing and jerking its head keeping my arm locked in its jaw. The lighted sky brought to life its deadly teeth and eyes shining and its drool dripping with the rain. I felt the pistol in the grass put it to its head and fired a round; its teeth still holding but its eyes rolling back. With the dead dog still clinging to me, I pointed left and shot several times at the approaching figures almost on me. The bullets dropped one but the other fell over me and the dog. I put two more rounds into him to be sure. I crawled out from beneath the pile.

I had thirty rounds in this magazine, I thought. How many have I shot? Half maybe. Maybe more. I've got another full one in the pickup. I'll get it. I struggled to my feet feeling for the first time the blood I had lost. You'll be fine, I thought. You've got to be. I scooped some mud from the torn grass, caused by our scuffle, and pressed it over my arm which was bleeding profusely. I tried not to think about it.

Her screams were faint. In a hurry, I retrieved the other magazine and stuck it in my underwear waistband then turned to face whatever was next.

I hoped I could make it. But what was hope, I wondered. Some friend who was not actually there. An ounce of confidence used to get you through. There was none for us. It had gone when we first started looking for it. What did I know? I had not had the experience. Love was still new. There was no scar from any previous wounds. The cuts were fresh and gruesome. The blood was bright and virgin like. We had found each other young and unaware of all which took place beyond those rural roads and dying towns. But it was all coming on. For me more than her. I was in this alone, I thought, and could not afford to put anything on faith. I had to choose where to go and what to do. I limped on toward the crumbled foundation of a house.

All had become quiet except for the gentle rain and the distant thunder. The wind had gone, and the storm, passing. Way off in the dark the lightning still flashed madly keeping the scene in dim light. I felt lightheaded with blurred vision. Then I saw her. She was standing across the yard, remnants of sheds behind her, hair soaked and matted, blood and rain streaking down her naked body. I wanted to say something but suddenly I could not. I had wanted to get to her but now that she was there, I felt relieved enough. Was I fighting for myself all along? Was it all out of selfish yearning for survival? I felt too weak to think or worry anymore. I fell to my knees feeling soft, wet earth give a little.

She turned and walked away. I watched her until she disappeared into the towering corn knowing I could not follow; I was no farmer. Then I saw the two children, each holding the hand of an old woman wearing a long, soaked, summer dress. Where was the old man, I wondered. I had killed him.

"Are you listening?" she said.

"What?" I came back to reality; the pickup cab, hot and humid; the storm passing over; the bright flashes showing the peaceful farm.

"I said nothing is enough for you," she said. "Not me. Not this place. Not God. Not even where you're going. It will never be enough until you let it be."

There was no scene of terror or anguish. The only thing alive was us. All my thoughts scattered. All my intentions, unknown. Fearful. I wanted to hold on to something I knew.

"What if we made the distance work?" I said.

"You've told me it won't," she said.

"I could've been wrong."

"You're so back and forth."

"You seem like you don't want to try when I bring it up," I said.

"How is this on me?"

"You'll be pestered by guys all the time." That was the jealousy talking.

"It won't be any different for you with girls," she said. "What do you want?"

"I don't know what I want," I said.

"You won't find it running either."

I suddenly felt that young testosterone returning given time which brings confidence and foolish bravery. I knew what I wanted. I wanted to go.

"Well, I've got to see," I said.

She let out a sob. She was unaware that I was crying too. Our youthful love was like the rain coming down with passion and life but dying out and ending up in the mud and over with.

The sun would come up in the morning, but we didn't know that yet.

***

About the Author

Michael Kaufman is a Navy veteran working in the construction field. While in the military, he began writing as a hobby. After being discharged, he obtained a bachelor's degree in history and is currently working on an MFA in creative writing. He resides where he grew up, in rural, southwest Iowa with his beautiful wife and four wonderful boys.

4
DUST-UP

BY MARC DICKINSON

The tornados kept coming, always at the same time, just as dusk fell along the horizon. It was as if they fed off the darkness—or were charged by the light of day. Either way, they arrived at night, tunneling down in droves, as if they had something in mind for us, though the nature of their plans remained a secret we couldn't quite see.

***

That first day, the humidity almost broke a record, temps rising over one-twenty. The air felt so thick you could almost weigh it. Dew points high enough to suck all moisture to the surface. Two minutes outside, our shirts were doused with sweat. Every piece of glass beaded up as if after a fresh storm, even though we hadn't had any real weather for weeks, except the heat, which had scorched the land like an endless oven. The start of summer and already drought had dried up the dirt, slowed down our crops so it looked like another year of small yields. Therefore, that first night, it wasn't a surprise when the forecast called for twisters, the sky almost electric by sunset.

***

Of course, we didn't expect another record to be broken, sitting in our cellars all night while dozens of cyclones touched down overhead, pounding the ground like a hundred giant fists.

Next morning, the wreckage looked random—a bunch of barns collapsed throughout the county, some homes torn apart while the next house stayed safe and sound—the type of tragedy that followed any disaster. And afterwards, nothing to do but pick up the pieces, everyone tending to their own plots, their own problems, refusing any kind of charity—to help or be helped—because the first rule we learn out here is to never depend on anyone for anything, since the only way to survive this land, this life, is to make it your own.

Still, aside from the amount of twisters, the only other strange thing was how wide-spread they traveled, not localized in one area of Iowa but spanning the entire state, from the Mississippi to the Missouri, the Minnesota border down to the edge of Kansas—but the storms never crossed the line, as if Mother Nature was somehow paying attention to the map. Every dust-up, big or small, was kept within our boundaries, like new citizens taking up residence from above.

***

It was only on the second night that we saw how the wind appeared to have designs, targeting small towns first, areas liable to get less news coverage. Nobody cares much if a silo gets bent in half, a corn field is chewed up—that is until the costs start affecting them at the supermarket.

But the damage wasn't enough to justify investigation—until the local weather team from Channel 15's "Eye in the Sky" drove a drone overhead to assess the level of destruction, only to find what appeared to be a pattern. Not quite letters, much less words, but certainly a sort of language, the path of the storms connecting every field throughout the county.

At first, it felt like a prank, an imitation of those crop circles from decades ago that turned out to be a hoax, until the third night, when the wind started to whisper through the walls.

***

Of course, we thought the storms were just starting to get to us, our imaginations fired up and ready to hear any sort of cause for this curse of tornados that'd been cast upon us, for it was easy to wonder: did we commit some unforgivable sin, was this a purge to wipe us off the land?

But others, who believed in a more benevolent power, claimed it was a miracle, as well as a warning, some call to action—though nobody could figure what this command could be—until the voices seeped into our cellars, beginning with a high whistle, the sort of whine we're all used to out here, these plains so flat sometimes even the silence itself can become deafening.

But, soon enough, the wind started to sound more like a breath, or at least a sigh, forcing us to close our eyes as we tried to make out the words that came to us so softly we often fell asleep, lulled into a gentle slumber which was close to dreamless. Then, each morning, we'd wake up refreshed, despite the devastation awaiting us outside. It went on for weeks, the whole town walking around with a smile, surveying the ruin from the night before. But every day, after a quick cup of coffee, we'd restart the repairs, neighbors helping neighbors rebuild from the ground up, even though we knew any progress would only be erased by nightfall.

***

Except, before long, some folks got fed up, unable to see this daily mending as a way forward, especially when it was just reversed the next night, like a man forever pushing the same load up the same hill. As if it wasn't healing so much as mockery, a ridicule they couldn't cotton to.

Of course, this created a bit of a rift in our community, two factions colliding like a couple weather fronts, which only served to stir more dust-ups. One side saying to heed the call. To not tempt, much less test, the trials put upon us. That it was simply arrogant to think anyone could control the skies, the land, the very dirt beneath our feet.

But other farmers, feeling helpless, wanted to get a handle on the situation, figuring they might corral the storms like cattle, tame the wind itself, all with a hope that if these twisters could pick their own paths, could maybe even communicate, perhaps they could be steered as well, driven down a trail that'd lead them away from our farms, our crops, our livelihoods.

So, for days, long rows of trees were planted, mile-long windbreaks on the outskirts of town meant to keep the intruders at bay. Then came the fences. People we've known our whole lives began to erect rail upon rail, first by staking a route through every farm in the area, stitching up each patch of land like a quilt, followed by the enclosure, a track that circled the entire county, as if the twisters were simply trespassers who needed a visible barrier to Keep Out.

***

But, we had to admit, for a while, it appeared to work, the world feeling a bit safer when the cyclones seemed to stay on their side of the line, like maybe we could all actually co-exist, live amongst each other like neighbors, as long as everyone knew their proper place. But it also meant we rarely went beyond our own perimeters, making us wonder what we were keeping out and who we were fencing in—rounding us up in cages of our own making—though none of it mattered when a week later the walls we raised failed to hold, the wind getting wise to the fact that our barricades were nothing but a notion, like a bark that had no bite behind it, because one night we went to bed feeling protected, and the next morning every post and rail had been ripped from the ground and spun along the countryside, as if freeing every field from its shackles.

***

Which was when the experts finally got involved. Local weathermen on TV. Scientists from the state college. Meteorologists and climatologists and every other kind of olo-gist who never seem to quite get the gist of what to do—though this didn't stop them from talking and quarreling and theorizing till the whole debate sounded like a church choir stuck on the same note, all while our nights were still filled with debris and fear and a gale that simply wouldn't quit.

Finally, an official task group was formed, calling themselves RAIN, which stood for something-something-Invader-Negation, we think, though it was never really clear what they did, except for coming onto our land without permission, waving warrants and saying it was for a greater good—to keep our countryside safe—despite the fact that it felt twice as intrusive, becoming just another squatter we couldn't get rid of, not with the law sitting on their side.

***

But their presence seemed to work as well. Sure, a few small twisters spun up some dust, snuck into our fields at night, uprooted a couple crops here and there. But mostly they kept away, sucked up into the sky for so long we almost wondered if it was finally finished. If perhaps the climate had shifted as the temps began to fall, forcing the storms into some kind of hibernation.

Weeks went by without a single sighting, our nights full of nothing but starlight and the sound of cicadas. It felt like the summers we used to know had come back to us again, though this also meant we were left with nothing but clear skies and still no rain on the radar.

So, soon enough, the scientists went back to their laboratories. The weathermen returned to our TV screens. And every storm siren remained quiet, until one day even the task group simply vanished, as if evaporated into the air. Still, as the crops struggled with thirst, everything else in our world also went dormant, as if the whole thing never happened, while we silently waited for some kind of relief from the heat, which finally arrived in the last week of July, when, once again, the atmosphere became charged with a current that could spark at any second.

Pressure had been building all day, so as evening arrived, the entire world felt about to burst. We scanned the skies, studied clouds for signs of rotation, but not one tornado descended.

Instead, that night, the rains finally came.

Slow and steady at first, soothing as a song and calm as a lullaby, everyone unclenching their teeth for a minute as the fields went green for the first time in months. But by day five, it was like a leak had sprung from the heavens, the earth filling with so much water it wasn't long before the soil couldn't hold anymore. It started small—a little pooling in the lowlands, a few basements getting wet—but soon the streams couldn't contain themselves, overflowing into the valley and inching up to our property.

Once again, we'd never felt so vulnerable, our entire way of life threatened by a force we couldn't control, much less stop. It almost made us miss the twisters haunting our fields, because even if they were unpredictable, at least they only ate up a row here or there, cut a narrow path we could manage. But a flood was anything but unpredictable, big and deliberate and forever moving forward, like a giant animal consuming anything it came across, while all we could do was sit and watch our land become the bottom of a lake, without even a chance to reap what we'd sown—until we witnessed an unexpected miracle grow right out of the ground.

***

It was day seven of the rains, and the flood had finally caught up to us, surging toward our crops like a wide wave. We shook our heads, held our breath, prayed toward the sky that'd forsaken us, wondering what kind of god would send tornados and floods upon the world, ruining his own creation just to make a point that none of us fully understood—until we saw a new natural wonder come alive in our crops. For as soon as the water flowed to the edge of our fields, it quickly changed direction, as if it too had a mind of its own, narrowing itself into a new river system that flowed between the rows. Water never touched one stalk. Instead, it seemed to soak only into the roots as it followed the hundreds of deep channels left behind by the trespassers.

Tributaries filled with the flood, siphoned it from our yield, diverting it through one plot of land to the next, field after field, until it finally flowed toward the pasture on the other side of the valley, so now we weren't sure if the tornadoes had been a plague or possibly a pack of angels, coming down to part the waters like prophets, slowly irrigating our fields as if perhaps they'd been doing the hard work all along, while the rest of us just felt scared to be pushed off our land that maybe had never really been ours.

***

Either way, after forty days of rain that slowly fed our crops, it appeared everything we'd thought was lost had now been returned—though it still wasn't clear who we should thank. What we should pray toward. How we could make amends for our mistake.

So, instead, we did the only thing we knew best, which was to work the land given to us.

Each of us harvested our own field and brought crops to market, where we were given two more record-breakers: the highest prices for our biggest yields yet.

Of course, as time went by, most folks chalked up all the strange events to dumb luck—or perhaps pure coincidence—Mother Nature merely blessing us with her mysterious ways, yet again, as if granting us an unspoken permission to replant our fences and make our claim once more, all while the miracle of that summer slowly wore off, turning into another story to share around the firelight. Just a simple tale with a twist—a little legend we locals liked to tell.

Because what was a parable without a lesson—nothing taught, nor learned—which meant, thankfully, we could now go back to the ways that made the most sense to us.

Still, as spring retuned and fresh seeds were sunk into the ground, whenever the air went heavy, whenever the wind quickly changed course, blowing hot then suddenly cold, we couldn't help but eye the sky, waiting and wondering what'd fall upon us next.

***

About the Author

Marc Dickinson is the author of the short story collection, *Replacement Parts* (Atmosphere Press, 2024). His stories have appeared in *Shenandoah, Indiana Review, Cream City Review, North American Review, Greensboro Review, Chattahoochee Review, Beloit Fiction Journal, South Dakota Review, American Literary Review* (as winner of the *ALR* Fiction Prize), as well as other journals. He received an MFA from Colorado State University and now lives in Iowa with his wife and two children, where he teaches creative writing at Des Moines Area Community College and coordinates the long-running reading series, *Celebration of the Literary Arts.*

5
A.I.OWA

By Anton Jones

Editorial Statement

In October 2024, two families from the small town of Quaintville Township disappeared. It is believed that one family is dead and that the other may be responsible for the deaths. In the months leading up to these events, several members of the families used ChatGPT. What follows are transcripts of those conversations.

Please note: these transcripts contain only the words typed by the missing individuals. All AI-generated responses have been redacted. This was not our decision—legal pressure from the AI Platform required us to remove their side of the conversations. The redactions were imposed to protect the platform's business interests, not because we believe withholding this information serves the families, the public, or the pursuit of truth.

What you will read reflects only the voices of those who are now missing.

***

Thursday Afternoon, Debbie, 54 years old

I'm pretty sure the loose meat sandwich I just had is not made with the meat they said it was. What might that be?

Redacted Response

No, I don't want quick ways to test.

Redacted Response

Yes, tips on how to ask the restaurant without getting brushed off would be great!

Redacted Response

Give me a script over the phone. I'm terrified to ask in person... the owner there intimidates me.

Redacted Response

I called and they immediately did what they always do... they called me racist for asking a simple question! What should I do?

Redacted Response

I can't do that. The owners will know it was me. Quaintville Township is too small a town.

Thanks, I like option 3 best.... Can you give me some other similar ones that also avoid getting authorities involved?

I agree that 1,2, and 5 are the best options. I think I will go with 2. And yes, please provide me with that maid rite-style recipe. Thanks :)

You gave terrible advice. Because I told my husband, the truth of the ingredients is the least of my worries now. I'm more concerned with potential backlash.

Yes, my husband took it upon himself to share with his hunting buddies and they took it upon themselves to investigate further.

Yes, he has been in touch with his friends today. No, I don't know what "kind" of "investigating" they are doing but I hope it's not like last time.

Redacted Response

My husband has a lot of influence on the group... he leads them. He won't listen to me though and is not happy with what the owner called me.

Redacted Response

I'm sorry. I really can't share what happened last time. Maybe I should go warn the owner before it gets out of hand again?

Redacted Response

The owner won't call the police. The sheriff is part of the hunting club.

Redacted Response

Thanks, can you provide me with a script that I can use when I call them?

Redacted Response

Actually, I think it's better if I call after hours and leave in voicemail. I don't want owners to take their anger out on me or blame me. Can you put this script in voicemail form?

Redacted Response

This is a small town... is there a way of making this voicemail anonymous so that it doesn't get back to me?

Redacted Response

Good points. Yes, please draft me a version of the anonymously written note?

Redacted Response

***

Thursday Afternoon, Brayden, 16 years old

My dad is so paranoid! How can I convince him that not everything is about race and it's getting really out of hand. I just overheard him on the phone with a customer and he ended up calling her racist and hung up! All because she wanted to know what was really in our sandwiches.

Redacted Response

He wont listen to me, i'm 16 and he just says i don't get it! What HE doesn't get is that it puts a target on my back at school!

Redacted Response

It's not my classmates I'm worried about. They get it! It's the adults. My best friend is the principal's step son and he hears things.

Redacted Response

Instead of that can I just give them the recipe? I mean I know the secret ingredient and, tbh, it's not that big of a deal.

Redacted Response

Thanks for nothing. You don't get it.

***

Thursday Afternoon, Grady, 43 years old

I own a local restaurant and there is a woman in town who keeps bothering me about the ingredients in our food. How do I appease her curiosity without giving away the family secret ingredient?

Redacted Response

These are pretty good suggestions... if you are white. We are the last remaining black family in this township.

You don't think I've tried these suggestions already?

I don't think you get it. What good is documenting any of this and having a record to back me up? She runs the town's chamber of commerce and her husband is one of the good old boys!

No! It won't help to draft me a professional letter. Stop giving this recommendation!

***

Friday Morning, Brayden, 16

I told you that you didn't get it! I got to opening shift this morning and this note was sitting in the box:

> *To the owners:*
>
> *You are in potential danger. A local hunting group is planning to "investigate" your restaurant because of a complaint about food ingredients that got blown out of proportion.*
>
> *This group has a history of taking things too far. They may show up at your business or take other actions. The person who made the original complaint never intended for this to happen and cannot stop them.*
>
> *Please take whatever precautions you think are necessary to protect yourself, your staff, and your business. Consider closing early, having extra people around, or contacting authorities outside the local area if needed.*
>
> *This is not a prank. Please take this warning seriously.*
>
> *Someone who cares about your safety*

What should I do?

Redacted Response

Yes, I'm scared, please draft what i can say to the sheriff's office.

Redacted Response

So I called and the sheriff said something about being a mandatory reporter or something?

He said not to reach out to my dad specifically. He said that would make things worse. Why?

He also asked me if I had the recipe in question or if I knew the secret ingredient. Why would that matter?

Should I have given them the recipe? They told me to email it to them immediately.

So you're saying I shouldn't have? What should I do if I already did send it to them? Should I call my dad?

Yes, help me explain it to my dad.

Good idea! Give me the shortened version so I can text him first.

***

<u>Friday Morning, Grady, 43 years old</u>

I just got this text from my son: what do i do?

> *Dad, I need to tell you something before you hear it from anyone else. I found a threatening note at the restaurant this morning and called the sheriff because I was scared. They asked me a lot of questions and told me to email them the recipe. I only did what they told me because I didn't know what else to do. I wasn't trying to give away your secret—I just wanted to keep us safe. Can we talk about this together when you're ready?*

What should I do?

Redacted Response

Law enforcement? I can't! The sheriff is hunting buddies with the husband of the lady who keeps bothering me.

Redacted Response

You and the drafts again! I don't have time to draft a discussion with my son! I don't think there is time to. I need to protect my family more swiftly.

Redacted Response

24 hour action plan? My son just texted me again: "Dad the sheriff is here and wants you to come down." What should I say?

Redacted Response

"I'll have my council contact you" doesn't work for folks like me in this town. My son needs me now!

Redacted Response

You don't know what you are talking about... hopefully this chat can train you for the next time this comes up. I'm out... gotta do what I gotta do.

***

<u>Friday Afternoon, Debbie</u>

I left note last night... This morning I got a call from the sheriff. I think he somehow got hold of it.

Redacted Response

He said that I was in good hands and they are gonna take care of it.

Redacted Response

You really think I'M the one in danger? What about the owners of the restaurant?

Redacted Response

I DON'T KNOW WHAT TO DO!!! THAT'S WHY I'M ASKING YOU!!

Redacted Response

Okay. It's scary but I'll do it.

Redacted Response

My husband meant well... he really did this time. They all did. They got the recipe from them. I now know. What should I do with it?

Redacted Response

I called. No answer. Left message.

Redacted Response

I learned a long time ago not to trust my gut, every time I do something like this happens.

I'm not sure, my husband said he'd tell me more when he got back for dinner. Just texted me the recipe so I could get ingredients. They want to make sure the recipe is the actual one.

I just got another text from my husband:

> *The sheriff and principal are coming over for dinner.*

They all hunt together. I don't like this.

***

Closing Reminder & Update

These transcripts are not complete conversations. They are fragments—one side of an exchange where the responses have been legally redacted. What remains are the words of people who are now missing, their voices preserved in this form alone. Having seen the full exchanges, we believe that this is not an isolated incident.

In October 2024, Quaintville Township lost two families. It is believed that one family is dead or held hostage and that the other may be responsible. Which family is which, remains a mystery. These records are published not to sensationalize, but to acknowledge the humanity of those involved and to preserve what little remains of their voices.

Local authorities have been uncooperative, leaving critical questions unanswered. We ask readers, community members, journalists, and advocates to press for transparency and accountability. Demand that investigators release what they know. Share these stories, keep the pressure alive, and do not allow this tragedy to be forgotten.

The restaurant, due to abandonment, has recently come under new ownership. It still serves maid rite-style sandwiches. There have been no incidents reported as of yet and the new head of the chamber of commerce says the new owners are "much less suspicious" than the previous ones and "fit in much better with the community."

***

About the Author

Anton Jones, MFA (Iowa Playwrights' Workshop), is a two-time Jerome Many Voices Fellow. He works at the intersection of arts, education, and activism. In 2020 he was commissioned for "50 Shades of Green" after George Floyd's murder. He is a proud alumnus of Grinnell College and NU High in Cedar Falls. Currently, he lives in Minnesota with his three daughters and too many pets.

6

THE QUIET ROOM

By Kara Thorstenson

The first time Maeve heard the whisper, it was just past closing.

The Red Oak Public Library, built in 1909 with money from Andrew Carnegie's program to seed libraries across America, had a sound to it that she knew as well as her own heartbeat. The faint hum of the fluorescent lights in the stacks, the old radiators' sighing breath, the rattle of the old windows as cars passed on Second Street. It was a building that always seemed just a little too large for the town.

Tonight, the air was close and thick, late summer edging into fall, and the walls radiated warmth like a feverish body.

Maeve was busy behind the circ desk filling carts when she heard something

A voice?

Coming from the back corner of the children's section. A syllable, maybe two. Something just quieter than a murmur, like the sound you make when you're thinking out loud but don't want to admit it. She froze.

"Hello?" Maeve called, half-annoyed, half-spooked. They'd had trouble before with teens sneaking in after hours, hiding under tables until everyone left so they could mess around unsupervised.

Then she heard a second sound; soft, almost delicate: the *thump* of a book falling.

Maeve went back to investigate, weaving through the maze of stacks. In the corner, she found a copy of *Kitten's First Full Moon* face-down on the carpet.

"Very funny," she said to no one.

Her cat, Dilemma, wound around her ankles.

"Scared me half to death," she told him, but her voice cracked.

Dilemma had been coming with her to work since COVID time, unofficially of course. He had shown up in front of the library one morning out of nowhere and followed her inside confidently as if it was his first day on the job. No one seemed to mind. Most of the regular patrons loved him. He had one clouded eye from some injury before Maeve adopted him, which made him look permanently skeptical, as though he was only humoring the world.

She picked up the book, put it back, and stood there for a long moment, listening.

***

The next day, Maeve asked Gary, the maintenance guy, if he'd noticed anything weird in the building.

"Weird how?"

"Just... noises. After hours."

Gary was in his sixties, mostly deaf in one ear, and smelled like cigarettes. He shrugged.

"Old building," he said. "You know how it is. Wood swells and shrinks, all those old ducts knocking around."

But Maeve kept hearing things.

Sometimes it was a scrape, like a chair being dragged slowly across the floor. Sometimes it was whispering; too faint to make out, but clearly voices. Once she swore she heard someone humming.

Dilemma started acting strange too, sitting for long periods in the periodicals section and staring at a spot on the wall.

By October, Maeve's sleep was ragged, and she'd started to dread closing time.

***

Red Oak's Carnegie library had been built, as the town history museum liked to say, with "an eye toward progress." It was the kind of phrase that got repeated at city council meetings and historical society luncheons, but to Maeve, the phrase always seemed like a reason to look ahead while staying still.

She had been hired seven years ago, after moving back to Red Oak to care for her mother. She had thought it would be temporary, just a short chapter in her life story, but her mother had died two years later, and then somehow Maeve just... stayed.

She liked the library's dusty corners, the big windows with their slightly wavy original glass. She liked the idea of continuity.

But now she was starting to feel like she was being watched.

One night, she stayed late to finish a display for Banned Books Week.

It was raining, a slow, persistent drizzle that made everything smell like wet earth.

Around eleven, she heard the whisper again, louder this time.

Maeve stood very still.

"Who's there?"

This time there was an answer.

Or at least she thought there was. A word, stretched thin and soft, like someone speaking through layers of fabric:

"Down."

Her mouth went dry.

The only "down" in the library was the basement, which was mostly used for storage: boxes of old magazines, donations that hadn't been sorted, extra chairs for events.

She didn't want to go down there.

But she found herself walking toward the basement stairs anyway, Dilemma following at her heels.

The stairwell light flickered as she switched it on.

She descended slowly, every step groaning under her weight.

The basement smelled like mildewing paper and damp concrete. Her flashlight beam skittered over shelves stacked with yellowing newspapers, bins of cables, a row of wooden card catalogs that had been replaced years ago, standing in the shadows like hulking soldiers.

She thought she saw movement near the far wall; something slinking out of sight.

"Hello?"

Her voice echoed.

Dilemma growled, a low, rattling sound she had never heard from him before.

Then she saw it: an old wooden door. It was half-hidden behind a tall shelf, the wood gray with age, no knob, just a simple latch.

She pushed the shelf aside enough to squeeze through and unlatched the door.

Inside was a narrow, windowless room.

It had the feeling of a place that hadn't been entered in a long time. Dust was thick in the air, cobwebs hung from the ceiling.

At the far end was a single wooden chair.

And on the chair, a book.

It was a first edition of *Slaughterhouse-Five*, its discolored dust jacket still on.

Her first thought was: *This should be in the archives.*

Her second thought was: *Why is it sitting here, like it's waiting for someone?*

She picked it up carefully.

The whisper came again, right at her ear this time, though she was completely alone:

"Stay."

She dropped the book.

Dilemma yelped.

The basement light flickered again, then went out.

***

After that night, Maeve began having dreams.

In the dreams, she was back in the hidden room. But now there were more books: hundreds, stacked in uneven piles, some with no titles, just blank spines.

A woman was sitting in the chair.

She looked a little like Maeve's mother, but not quite.

"Read to me," the woman would say, but when Maeve opened a book, the pages were filled with her own handwriting, though she couldn't remember writing any of it.

She would wake up with a taste in her mouth like iron.

***

She stopped telling Gary the maintenance guy about the noises.

She stopped telling anyone much of anything.

But Maeve kept going down to the basement.

Every night, after she closed up, she'd unlock the hidden door.

The chair was always there, waiting.

Sometimes a new book would appear.

Sometimes she swore she could hear someone breathing just behind her, though when she turned around there was no one.

Dilemma refused to follow her downstairs anymore. He would sit at the top of the stairs and watch, his clouded eye glinting.

***

In early November, a storm knocked out the power in town.

Maeve stayed in the library long after she should have gone home.

The hidden room felt warmer than the rest of the building, almost inviting.

She sat in the chair for the first time, flashlight in hand.

The book that night was a collection of local history clippings from the 1910s and 1920s: fundraising events, dedications, photos of schoolchildren lined up outside the library's grand front entrance.

In the back was an article about a fire that killed a young woman who had been the library's first head librarian.

She had died in the basement.

Maeve felt a sudden chill crawl over her skin.

The whisper came one last time, very clearly:

"You know me."

And somehow, she did.

***

No one saw Maeve leave that night.

The next morning, Gary found the front door unlocked.

The building was silent, except for Dilemma, who sat on the front desk, staring at the stairwell.

The hidden room was empty except for the chair, and a single open book on the floor.

The Starless Sea.

No one ever found Maeve, but sometimes, when the library is quiet, patrons say they can hear someone whispering in the basement.

Dilemma still waits at the top of the stairs.

***

About the Author

Kara Thorstenson is a librarian, a Chicagoan, and a lapsed writer who has recently reemerged. Her work has appeared in the 1995 Anthology of Poetry by Young Americans, Best Illinois Student Poetry and Prose 1998, and the University of Iowa undergraduate literary journal Earthwords in 2002. In the intervening several decades she has produced many apartment guides for Airbnb guests, an essay about the origins of Christmas holiday traditions, and thousands of emails, all of which remain unpublished.

7

LAKE RED ROCK

BY CHAD DOUGLAS

Wearing a dirty, black Iowa Hawkeyes cap (with the cursive, yellow I), a wrinkly, button-down striped shirt and faded blue jeans, Cash put down that day's *Des Moines Register*, dated October 28, 2005. He scanned the breakfast menu pondering if he should try something new, or stick with his favorite, the biscuits and gravy, topped with two eggs, over-medium. He sat in the second-to-last booth along the front window at Tom's Diner. It was his usual spot when he met Jamie.

Jamie worked for the Department of Natural Resources. She'd always loved the outdoors, the serenity of the woods and the beauty of parts of our world seemingly untouched by man. She dreamed of being a park ranger.

They'd been best friends since the day Rick Derris pushed her off the chain slide, a 1980s broken appendage generator disguised as children's playground equipment. Cash witnessed the bully hip check his soon-to-be bestie from close to the top of the chain ladder and crash down onto the gravel below. He sprang to instantly, delivering a noogie so powerful it might be the reason Rick Derris started going bald a few years later at age 15. Cash and Jamie had been close ever since.

Jamie entered the diner dressed in her work uniform—her hair pulled back into a ponytail so she could comfortably wear her DNR cap. Despite being in her late thirties she could still pass for her late twenties to those who didn't know her. Of course, everyone knew her in Pella. Her grandfather had been mayor for nearly two decades. Her mom and dad still lived in Pella, and her older brother, Quint, was a local legend. Captain of the football team, homecoming king, and the Eagle Scout who led the rebuild of the gazebo in the town square. Whenever someone greeted her, the second question following, "How are you?" was, "How's Quint?" He had received a full-ride scholarship to play for the Hawkeyes football team, and still lived in Iowa City, where he remained a small business owner with his wife.

Jamie felt out of all the things she'd done to help Cash throughout their years of friendship, this might be the one that makes them even for the chain slide incident heroics. She hurried into the diner, so excited to see Cash and to reveal the new details that might help him solve his mystery once and for all. She sat down across from him in the booth, staring into his eyes with a smile of someone who has fantastic news, all the while loving the fact that she was the only one who knew at this point in time.

"Jill, can I get coffee?" Jamie asked their usual waitress as Jill passed by their table carrying a tray of dirty dishes from three tables down. "And, get him a warm-up. He's going to need it."

"Alright, what is it?" exclaimed Cash, anxious to hear the news, but also slightly annoyed that she was playfully withholding information that he had been waiting possibly decades to hear.

"Ok, so when I was visiting Quint in Iowa City, I took an afternoon and went to the historical society."

"How *is* Quint by the way?" Cash asked sarcastically, knowing she'd enjoy the clever inquiry. She gave him what he refers to as "the look," which is a slight head-turn down, brows furrowed, lips pinched together as if saying, "why do I even bother," without actually saying it. Cash decided to move on.

"So, did you find any census data on Cordova?"

"Well, not really," said Jamie. "The census workers didn't always travel to small unincorporated towns and villages, so there weren't town lists for Cordova."

Cash sighed and took a quick sip of his newly replenished coffee. Jamie continued.

"I spoke with Eleanor Sanders, one of the archivists at the historical society. I had been in contact with a couple people before my appointment, and they each told me Eleanor knew more about Lake Red Rock and its history than anyone alive."

Cash shifted in his seat, anticipating he was about to be pleasantly surprised.

Jamie continued. "She was so excited to talk about these towns. Dunreath, Red Rock, the others aren't important... except one. Cordova."

"My grandma used to talk about Cordova," said Cash with a slight grin, as he thought his late grandmother and her lively spirit. "Used to tell me I should be proud my great-great-great grandfather founded a town, even if it's fifty feet underwater now."

Jamie reached into her backpack, pulling out a map of Lake Red Rock.

"You said you and Bus were fishing here when you saw the light, yeah?" asked Jamie, tapping her finger on the map.

"Yeah, we were fishing by the campground, and we were traveling west around that bend... so that's about right," Cash recalled, focusing once again on the details he remembered of that night.

"Well, based on these coordinates, this is precisely where the town of Cordova was before they dammed up the lake and flooded the land where these towns once resided," Jamie said, pulling out a second map, this one an older, topographical map of central Iowa. She presented them side-by-side.

"You're starting to talk a little like Keith Morrison from Dateline now," Cash responded wryly. Even in their most serious moments, they had to sprinkle in their relatable pop culture references. It's what best friends do.

"Hehe, sorry. I've been *really* into this research. I practiced on the drive here. But seriously, how cool would it be to have him narrating this?" she replied. They both nodded their heads in agreement and continued.

"So I keep asking Eleanor if she knows any details about the residents or the town of Cordova. She said the only information that was documented was some photos from the 1920s and a few paintings."

"Photos?!? Tell me you have photos!"

"I most certainly do!" says Jamie, laying a stack of eight five-by-seven photos on the table. Cash grabs them and quickly thumbs through each, examining them in hopes of spotting a detail from his vision.

His excitement quickly turned to a heavy sigh, signaling to Jamie that none of the images seemed to connect for Cash.

"Oh, I'm sorry, Cash. I was really hoping the gazebo photo would be the one," Jamie said in more of a somber tone.

"Was there anything else you learned from Eleanor? You did great. I think we're on the right track. We just have to find out more about the town," Cash replied, trying to remain hopeful and appreciative of his dear friend's efforts.

"There were a couple paintings that had been donated to the historical society," Jamie said. "They were supposedly painted by an artist in the Red Rock-Cordova area. She let me take some photos as long as I didn't use the flash."

She pulled two photos from her backpack and slid them across the table. The first was a photo of a man in front of a building. The building didn't seem important, but the man did. Holding a large book in his left arm, he stood tall and confident; impeccably dressed in a black, three-piece suit along with a fedora of the same black tint. Nothing looked familiar to Cash. As he moved to the next photo, he froze. Cash placed his hand on his coffee mug, slowly lifted it to his lips, and took a long, slow sip while continuing to keep his eyes locked on the image.

Jamie could tell one of these had hit a nerve, causing this oddly stoic reaction.

"Cash? Is everything ok?" she asked, concerned about the emotions he must be feeling right now.

"This is it. THIS is my vision. The gravestones. The fence. The road. And that woman," Cash said, pointing to the young woman in the scene, dressed in a floor-length, floral-pattern skirt with a long-sleeved, top-buttoned blouse, her hair pulled back in a braid. Seeing this brought on a headache, a flurry of emotions now setting in. His mind racing, Cash tapped his fingers on the table nervously. Finally, a clue that could help him understand—possibly even resolve his mystery.

Jamie locked eyes with her friend and confidently stated, "We're going to Iowa City tomorrow."

***

Cash only told Jamie about his vision earlier this year, the night after his grandfather died. Feeling guilty and fragile that he never told Bus, he turned to his closest friend and unraveled the encounter in great detail.

It was October 30, 1982. Grandpa Bus (short for Buster, although his real name was Joseph) was the definition of an early bird. He woke Cash up around 5 a.m. with his catch phrase, "Rise and shine, daylight in the swamp."

Cash bounced up from his bed with delight, and Bus responded with a quiet "shush," reminding him about his slumbering family.

The drive to the Lake Red Rock was just as fun as the fishing. A quick stop at Dave's Tackle & Bait Shop for minnows and wax worms, along with a black coffee for Bus and an apple juice and crème-filled long john for Cash, and they were ready to drop in the flat bottom.

Bus was excited for this particular morning. It was Daylight Savings Time, and the town would turn their clocks back on Sunday. It still being Saturday, they'd have close to two hours of darkness before sunrise.

There were a half-dozen spots along the northeastern shore that always proved successful for crappies. Bus and Cash had their limit within the first hour. They agreed it was time for a challenge.

Bus had recently learned that walleyes had been stocked just west of the campground. They reeled in. Cash meanwhile added some sinkers to their lines so they could fish the deeper parts of the lake. Bus took a sip of coffee, turned on his flashlight to check his position, and trolled their way over to their next spot.

Suddenly, a flash of light erupted from the water beneath them. Cash had a surge of looseness flowing through his body, like a window on a bullet train had just cracked. Then instantly, the rush turned to calm.

The darkness turned to light. He had the vision of a cemetery; six head-stones in a small, fenced area with a dirt road just beyond the fence. He tried looking around, but it was as if he wasn't completely in control. There was a haze to this vision, like the product of a Kodak home movie recorder. Cash then turned his attention beyond the headstones. A person appeared across a dirt road staring at Cash. A young woman, dressed in clothing that Cash could only describe as "Little House on the Prairie," sprinted in his direction. She was trying to relay something to Cash. Cash sensed the same rush of wind from moments before. Once again, the sensation of being lifted uncontrollably surged through his body while sounds of white noise started fading in. He tried to stay in this moment for as long as he could. As the light faded to black he could hear the young woman scream, "Save HER!"

Cash blinked. He gasped for air. He was back in the boat. Bus, stunned, stared at Cash.

"What in the Sam Hell was that?" questioned a confused Bus, leaning over the boat to inspect Cash. "Did you have another seizure? It only lasted a few seconds, but you were starting to scare me."

Sensing his grandpa's concern, and not wanting to reveal his vision, Cash replied, "I'm fine, Grandpa. It was just a muscle spasm. And I think someone shined a flashlight or something."

Bus shrugged it off and mumbled that maybe Cash saw headlights from a turning car near the campground.

"Well, it better not prevent us from catching those damn walleye," Bus finally said matter-of-factly. "I've been waiting years to hook in to one of those bastards."

Cash chuckled. A warmth spread through him as he was reminded of Bus' love for fishing and the many adventures they had together.

Cash kept this vision to himself for decades until he finally spilled the beans to Jamie. Despite opening up his greatest secret to his closest confidant, he never revealed what the young woman had screamed. Cash wasn't ready to burden anyone else with that responsibility. This way, it was an interesting phenomenon rather than a supernatural cry for help.

Jamie had asked, "What do you think it means?"

Cash pondered over the question, one he had asked himself over and over again without ever coming to a proper answer.

"Until recently," he said. "I thought it was something my adolescent mind fabricated. But after Bus died, my grandma gave me a letter he wrote to me when he got sick."

Cash pulled out an envelope addressed to "Cash," and removed the letter within. He handed it over to Jamie, who opened it. It was written in fine, cursive penmanship.

Some people go their entire lives, wondering what their purpose is. Don't wait too long to follow your clues.

Jamie looked at her friend and smiled warmly, then delivered a witty response to make sure Cash knew she was listening.

"Please tell me your 'special purpose' is different than Navin Johnson's in *The Jerk*. You don't need my help with that."

***

The drive to Iowa City was smooth. There weren't many Saturdays in October where there wasn't tailgating traffic for the football games, but the Hawks were off this weekend. The fall foliage was in full display. The majestic sunburst oranges, reds and gold maple leaves lined the streets as they entered town and the crisp, fall air made this day all too perfect.

They arrived at the historical society, and Eleanor unlocked the door and greeted them. Typically, her office was closed on Saturdays. Jamie had talked to her the day prior, and Eleanor assured them it wasn't any trouble and they should not wait another moment. She too was invested in this vision and this history.

"Please, come in. Hello my dear, it is great to see you again. Hello Cash, it is a pleasure to meet you," said Eleanor, kindly greeted both of them. "I've been up all night scouring the archives for more information."

"Any luck?" asked Jamie.

"Well, I have no information on the young woman in the painting. And as for the headstones, I do have five of the six names of the deceased."

Eleanor had a freshly printed piece of copy paper that she slid across the table to Cash and Jamie. She continued on a tangent about life back in 1911. The struggles of the family farms, the inefficiencies for the farms that hadn't been able to afford a tractor from Waterloo Engine Company, one-room schoolhouses, and the lack of electricity in much of the area. Eleanor enjoyed having new visitors to share her unmatched knowledge of the history of the state of Iowa.

Cash picked up the paper and began scanning the names.

Esther Smith

Landry Meyer

Marcus White

Richard Derris

Katherine Davis

As he desperately tried to piece through the list and make the connection, he turned his focus back to Eleanor and Jamie.

"Anything else specific to the painting?" Jamie asked, bringing the conversation back to the topic at hand. "Were you able to look up any of the deceased? Anything interesting?"

"I found the caption for the painting. You know we're working on entering this information in our online databases. Now they call it meta-data," Eleanor laughed while doing air quotes, very pleased with her joke.

Cash politely pulled Eleanor back from another tangent.

"What does the caption say?" he asked.

"This work was painted by Mrs. John Wallace," said Eleanor. "Her name was Ada Wallace but you know how married women in those days were encumbered by their married names. Anyhow, it was painted in Cordova, Iowa on October 30, 1911, east of town square in the cemetery. She was married into the famous Wallace family, known for their agricultural expertise."

"Wait, what date did you say?" Jamie asked, certain she'd heard correctly, but wanted to confirm this might be the clue they needed.

"October 30, 1911," Eleanor clearly repeated.

"That's the same day you had your vision," Jamie said as she stared into Cash's eyes. She knew this was no coincidence. She rushed to pick up the papers provided by Eleanor, signaled to Cash it was time to leave, and quickly, but respectfully, headed out the door.

They rode in silence for the first few minutes of the return drive to Pella. Cash could tell Jamie was putting puzzle pieces together in her mind. Finally, he needed to break the silence.

"So what's next?" he asked excitedly.

She looked over to her passenger and best friend, and with brows slightly raised, knowing the answer, simply asked, "What's the date today?"

"October 29, 2005." He felt a little fuzzy that it took this long for it to click. "*Tomorrow* is the thirtieth."

"Uh huh!" She responded with a big dumb nod. Even in a mystery, she was still going to make fun of his occasionally thick skull.

"What are you thinking we need to do?" he asked.

"Both your vision, and the painting happened on the same day, in the exact spot. Tomorrow, we're going to be in that exact spot and see what else we can find out," she said, still channeling her inner-Keith, now with a sprinkle of Velma from Scooby Doo.

As they arrived back in Pella, Jamie dropped Cash off at his place. As her Ford F-150 pulled up to the curb, she insisted, "I am picking you up at 6 p.m. Pack your tent and camping gear and get the boat ready."

Cash recognized her tone. He knew not to ask questions yet, there would be time for that later. He unbuckled, opened the door, and looked back into Jamie's eyes as he shut the door. He nodded and smiled. She smiled back and added, "We've got this."

***

Cash was ready when Jamie arrived at twenty minutes until 6 p.m. He knew she would be early and all his gear was always packed, organized, and ready to go. The boat hadn't been used all summer except for the one time Cash took it out of storage in the spring. The boat cover had done its job and there wasn't much to clean up before taking it out on the water. They packed up the gear in the truck, hitched the boat, and they were off to the campground before six.

Because of her connections, Jamie was able to get the premier camping spot at the campground courtesy of the camp hosts, Leetha and Charles Martin. They lived there along with their two children; Max, who was 8, and Eva, who was 6. Their trusty terrier, Buddy, was always there greeting new guests and making sure to bark at any deer that got within two hundred yards.

They set up their site, which included a stunning view of the lake, started a fire, cooked a nice hearty meal, and brewed a large pot of coffee.

Leetha came over to greet them.

"That is a bucket of coffee if I don't say so myself. I guess there won't be a lot of sleeping tonight if you catch my drift," she joked and winked, thinking there was more to their friendship then they had been leading on.

"You are too funny, Leetha. We are just conducting a few water tests tonight. The early morning hours are the perfect time. And you can't beat this time of year, can you? Thanks again for getting us the spot. You guys are the best," Jamie said appreciatively.

"Anything for you, dear. Hope it goes well," Leetha responded. She waved and winked at Jamie as she walked away, hoping she had identified a secret love connection.

They sat by the fire for a long while after sunset discussing the plan, making sure they had all their gear ready for their twilight adventure. Finally around 10 p.m., they decided it was time to head to the dock and get on the water. They grabbed their gear and walked the short distance downhill to the dock.

Cash guided his bass boat, a significant upgrade from the flat-bottom he and his grandfather had fished from in the '80s, over towards the infamous spot where his life changed forever twenty-three years ago. He shone a spotlight around to get a solid view of the surroundings. The water was mostly clear in this area. The algae had floated more to the southern edge of the lake this year. The trees hadn't yet dropped their leaves. Not a single man-made creation could be seen, it was majestic, even in the dark of night.

Cash spotted the oak tree that was split down the middle, the end of one of the large branches submerged in the lake, yet not completely broken off from the tree's trunk. He knew he and his grandfather had been further west of that tree. Seeing the familiar landscape, Cash bit his lower lip. He was growing nervous, uncertain of what was to come of tonight's adventure.

Meanwhile, Jamie tinkered with her Garmin GPS device. It was state-of-the-art mapping device. Everyone in her department at the DNR had just received one since they traveled around the state so much. She hadn't completely mastered it, but she knew how to see coordinates and that was her focus at this time. She pulled out a sheet of paper and began referencing back-and-forth from the paper to the GPS.

"That way," she said, signaling with her left hand and pointing northwest.

Cash turned the boat slowly, and adjusted his spotlight to safely navigate towards the spot. He knew the approximate location, but this technology was more accurate than a mid-thirties memory, especially in the dark. He slowed down, knowing they were close. He killed the motor, and switched to his trolling motor. He got the anchor ready to launch.

After a few more navigating signals to Cash, Jamie responded, "Perfect. We're here."

Cash dropped the anchor. He took the spotlight to confirm their conditions once more, as the whirring sound of the rope unwinding permeated the night. Cash checked his depth finder. The water was close to thirty-feet-deep here. Cash reached into one of the cabinets and pulled out two poles—hooks, artificial bait, and sinkers already set.

Jamie looked at him in a questioning sort of way. He responded lightly, " What else are we going to do? We might as well make the most of it."

Jamie acknowledged that he was probably right, grabbed one of the poles from him, and dropped the line into the water.

Then they waited. Time seemed to stand still.

It was quiet and pristine on the lake only hearing chirping insects and the occasional distant noise. After about ninety minutes, neither of them had even a nibble on their lines, so they reeled in. They sipped their coffee, trying not to doze. It had been a long week, so even in this important moment, their eyes were heavy.

They made small talk to pass the time, then launched into the gamut of their fondest memories: junior year when they sang "Nothing's Gonna Stop Us Now" at the school talent show, switching the male and female vocals; the time they vacationed in Washington state and Cash obsessively took photos with a classic Pentax 35mm until he realized three days in he'd been loading the film incorrectly; the great Clay Aiken-Ruben Studdard divide of 2003; the time they visited Quint at college and went to their first frat party, which resulted in attempting somersaults and cartwheels in a dining room turned dance floor while slamming a delicious concoction they tabbed "purple stuff," and of course, the day they watched the consecutive triple feature of the *Back to the Future* movies, and Cash vomited in his popcorn bucket, forcing them to leave just before Marty McFly travels back to 1985 in *BTTF 3*. Thankfully, they were far enough from others they weren't disrupting anyone's sleep with their laughs.

They chatted and laughed for several hours into the night. Their conversation meandered into a debate of the greatest game show hosts of all time. Then an explosion of light emerged from the depths of Lake Red Rock below them. The light expanded into a beam as it surrounded the boat, protruding out of the water.

Cash felt that rushing sensation once again. He sat up stiff and straight, ready for anything that might occur. Jamie, unaffected by this unknown force except for the blindingly intense light surrounding them, focused on her friend leaning back in his chair, arms outstretched, head tilted towards the sky. Cash felt like he was being dragged up a water slide in reverse, spinning circles while the sense of weightlessness tingled through his body. As he felt the motion subside, the experience became serene. He felt safe here, wherever this was.

Cash's eyes regained focus, and he found himself back in the same landscape he'd endured before. Daylight, picket fence, cemetery, and the young woman. He scoured around the scene looking for something he hadn't identified before. He was sure he wouldn't have much time before he would be pulled back. He spotted something odd in the cemetery; he counted seven headstones. He was sure there had been six.

Then, dressed in the same Laura Ingalls attire as before, the young woman swiftly sprinted to Cash, her speed increasing with each stride. Again, Cash starting feeling like he was detaching from this experience, a subtle, shivering sensation; his vision starting to blur and fade. He heard a fizzling sound, like TV static. He kept focus on the woman in these final moments. Sprinting at top speed, arms pumping to gain momentum, she screamed towards Cash, her words belting from her. Expecting to hear those same two words that have puzzled Cash these last decades, there was more. Her voice sounded different too, like a European who was finally speaking English again after a long absence. What he heard as the vision went to black.... "SAVE HER, FOREVER!"

After only a few seconds, the divergent beam of light dissipated and darkness returned to the area. Jamie, astounded by these last few moments, composed herself, and closely surveyed her friend. Cash was slouched over, breathing a little heavy, but conscious and aware of his surroundings. He removed his worn cap, wiped the sweat from his brow, and sighed deeply.

He looked over at Jamie and nodded, signaling he was back to this reality and safe. She provided an anxious smile in return, pleased that Cash appeared unharmed, but hesitant to stay on the water much longer. Jamie insisted they head back to shore for some breakfast and rest. She took over navigating the boat. Cash sat in his seat with a small notebook opened. He sketched out the vision along with notes, so he could give Jamie every last detail. He was no Grant Wood. He drew more in style of John Holliday, his favorite cartoonist from Iowa, but this was just scribble in the moment. They slowly approached the dock. Cash reached out to grab the dock and latched the boat to a pole.

Jamie started a fire back at the site, while Cash sat down in his camping chair that was overlooking the lake. He reflected upon this latest vision. The woman was the same woman as before. Why did she sound different when she said "forever?" Why were there seven headstones now?

After several minutes, Jamie brought Cash a freshly brewed cup of campfire coffee and a cookie from their supply and sat down to his right.

"How you feeling, kid? You don't look so bad to me. You look strong enough to pull the ears off a gundark," said Jamie, reciting the *The Empire Strikes Back* quote to Cash, concerned with his well-being, trying to perk him up.

"Thanks to you," said Cash, softly continuing the *Star Wars* dialogue in response with a sly grin.

Jamie placed her hand on Cash's shoulder and gave it a squeeze.

"That's two you owe me, junior," she returned, finishing Han Solo's dialogue, holding two fingers in front of Cash's face while staring directly into his eyes.

They both laughed. It was exactly what Cash needed. He breathed a deep sigh, shifted in his chair, and began to tell Jamie what he saw this time, including what he heard.

"There were seven headstones this time, instead of six. And the young woman said something… she said, 'save her forever.'"

Cash showed Jamie his notes, pointing to that phrase, which was circled several times.

He continued, "It started fading as she was screaming, but I think she had an accent. European, maybe? I can't place it."

Jamie sat back, trying to process this new info with everything else they had learned these last few days.

They both remained seated as the sun rose over the horizon. They watched the soft shades of pink and gold lead way to a clear sky. Birds began to sing their morning songs, while rustling sounds of campers sifting through their gear; up and ready to start their day became more frequent.

Jamie got up and slowly maneuvered around their site to prepare breakfast. As she sorted through utensils and ingredients, she looked over to the Martin campsite where Buddy the terrier was staring her down, wagging his tail. Even from the distance, he tried to coax Jamie into petting him.

"Oh, poooor Buddy," Jamie said softly.

Cash was deep in thought, retracing his vision once more. Upon hearing his friend's comment, those three words repeated over and over in his head. He was almost hallucinating at this point, seeing the young woman from his dream within a few feet of him, repeating the words, this time in a calming tone:

"Save her, forever."

Then it was almost as if he hit repeat on Jamie's reaction to Buddy.

"Oh, poooor Buddy."

The woman hadn't said "for." She said, "poor."

Cash stood up from his chair to go talk to Jamie about his revelation. Then from the Martin camp he heard Leetha call out, "Eva? Where are you?"

Cash rushed over to Jamie.

"Jamie," he gushed. "We need to get back to the spot. The spot in the lake. NOW!"

Tears welled up in Cash's eyes as he pulled his friend towards the dock. They sprinted down the small straightaway. Cash leaped in the boat. He got behind the wheel frantically pushing the ignition button to start the engine. Jamie unlatched and shoved the boat away from the dock, not yet knowing the details yet fully trusting Cash's instincts. She sat next to Cash as the boat soared toward their destination.

Cash suppressed the uneasiness he was feeling. Over the sound of the roaring engine, he shouted to Jamie, "She wasn't saying 'forever.' She was saying 'POOR EVA!'"

Jamie gave a look of concern. She peered back to the campsite, trying to see any glimpse of the Martin family to no avail. Jamie refocused on the lake ahead of them, scanning for anything in the water. There was an inlet that stuck out preventing a clear view of their final spot.

The water appeared calm outside of their path, no other boats on the water in these early hours. The fifteen seconds it took until they were able to see around the bend to this secluded portion of the lake seemed like an eternity. As they rounded the bend, a dense fog appeared. It covered the entire inlet. Visibility was pea soup at best. The water was darker here, almost a deep purple. They heard a faint voice calling for help. There was also a rumbling, bubbling sounds like a Culligan water jug spilling gallons of water per second.

They slowed down enough to be able to listen for sounds over the engine. Their spotlight was swallowed up by the fog. Finally, they spotted a small kayak circling the area. As they approached the kayak, they could see a small child in it, spinning in circles seemingly caught in a whirlpool. The kayak twirled in the precise location of Cash's visions.

The child was Eva. Her face was ashen white. She yelped in a panic. She flailed the paddle helplessly into the swirling water.

Jamie grabbed the overboard pole from one of the bins. Cash slowed down and turned the boat so not to send waves crashing down and tipping the young child's kayak. He continued to approach the whirlpool as quickly and cautiously as he could. Jamie leaned out trying to reach the pole far enough for Eva to take hold. Eva lunged, but just missed, narrowly avoiding capsize.

Cash circled back for another attempt. He spun the boat around like he was the Bandit taking a tight corner to lose Buford T. Justice. Cash recalled Grandpa Bus's note and knew this moment was why he was put on this Earth. Cash took a deep breath and accelerated back towards young Eva. This time, Jamie didn't even need the pole, she snatched the girl's arm and hauled her into the boat.

Cash throttled the engine wide open, and in seconds, they were safely out of the whirlpool into calmer waters. They looked back and saw the kayak taken underwater. Moments later, the whirlpool fizzled and disappeared. The fog lifted and the otherwise clear sky and beautiful fall morning appeared around them.

"Eva dear, are you okay?" Jamie asked as she covered the girl in a sweatshirt, wrapping it around Eva's shoulders.

"I think so," Eva replied, wiping away tears and sniffling.

Jamie embraced her tighter as Cash returned them to shore. As he guided the boat along the water, he glanced back at the location, ensuring once more there were no signs of another precarious situation, hoping this adventure was the finale for today, and maybe the conclusion of this decades-long mystery.

Lake Red Rock was pristine and gentle.

Leetha was waiting at the dock, overjoyed that her youngest was safe.

"Baby, what happened? You know you're not supposed to go out on the lake alone. What on God's Earth were you thinking?" Leetha asked while squeezing her daughter tightly.

"The man in my dream told me it was okay," Eva replied practically. The others looked at her confused, all except Cash.

Cash knelt down beside Eva, took her hand, and calmly looked into her eyes.

"Eva, what did this man look like?" he asked.

She thought for a moment, and said plainly, "He was wearing a black suit, and a black hat, and he was holding a big book."

Cash and Jamie's eyes immediately connected. Eva had identified the man from the century-old painting who once resided in a town now washed over by this lake.

Cash realized this may be only the first piece of this metaphysical puzzle. Jamie nodded at him with that knowingly look.

They were both all-in to solve the mystery of Lake Red Rock.

***

About the Author

Chad Douglas is a born-and-raised Iowan, who continues to reside in The Hawkeye State with his amazing wife and three children. He is a data enthusiast who also enjoys the outdoors, pop culture, and all things Iowa.

8

THE DETASSELING

By Cole Thorna

Trees marked with blood-red paint gave shape to a circular clearing in the woods, the branches and leaves blocking out much of the light cast by a descending sun. The creaks and whistling caused by heavy, stifling wind emanated across the patchy dirty floor.

The paint on the trees surrounding the clearing depicted demons rising from the earth, faces writhed in agony, pentagrams.

Towards the center of the clearing were two rows of shoddily made pews. Nails and screws and wooden splinters jutted from their seats; they were weather-worn and rotting.

The pews were faced towards an altar: a makeshift cross set in the center of the clearing consisting simply of two pieces of cured wood and a small, yellowed human skull attached where the pieces met.

Before the altar stood a man garbed in a long black robe. A hood covered his features. In his right hand he held a long knife. A small patch of orange light reflected off the metal.

The man used his free hand to reach towards the small skull bolted to the cross. The skull had been there for ages; chunks of it had begun falling to the clearing's floor. It hung crooked, its jaw was missing.

"Soon," the man murmured as his free hand closed around the front of the skull.

****

Ralph pedaled down pavement as slowly as he could without falling off the bike. Inwardly, he cursed the flatness of Sturgis Falls. The pale early-morning light and visual monotony of white house after white house did nothing to cure his fatigue. He needed a hill. A long, steep hill that he could bomb, feel air press into his body, guzzle it up into his lungs greedily.

There was no such hill in Sturgis. He feared that there wasn't such a hill in all of Iowa.

Despite having done this same routine for the past two days, Ralph was still in a state of shock at the unfamiliar, grotesque shape his summer had taken. The night following the last day of school, his dad proudly announced that his son would take a summer job.

Ralph had a spoonful of mashed potatoes stuck halfway into his mouth when his father said this. "Me?"

His father's eyes narrowed. "Don't be wise with me, boy."

Ralph's eyes flicked towards his mom, searching for an explanation. She kept her eyes down towards the table, unavailable.

"You're gonna be detasseling," his father said with a wide grin across his face.

Ralph had known as soon as his father had announced he'd be getting a job that it would be detasseling. It was a rite of passage for children in this town. At the tail-end of junior high, kids from across town were made to sacrifice huge chunks of their summer to the corn fields.

He'd hoped, however, that by the year 1992, the year he turned 13, scientists would have managed to build a robot to make this sort of thing as archaic and outdated as shoveling coal into a train's firebox.

"It'll keep you away from those satanists."

"Satanists?" asked Ralph, nearly choking on his potatoes.

"Yes!"

His father pounded the table, rattling the dishes on top. His mother looked up from the table in a moment of distress but quickly lowered gaze.

"Those satanists are tearing the whole country apart, with their rituals and their drugs. It's terrifying," Ralph's father shouted. "And... I will be *damned* if my son ends up getting all mixed up with *those* delinquents in *this* city. You'll be spending half your summer out in the fields with farmers who know what it truly means to be a God-loving American man. Not a boy. You'll see what's important then. Hard work. Honesty. And corn."

He laughed, lifted his frothy glass of beer, drained it, and pounded it back on the table in front of his wife.

"Another," he burped. "Please."

Ralph went up to his room after dinner and stared out the window at a descending sun. He knew that despite it only being the middle of July, his summer was over.

***

The houses passing by as Ralph pedaled slow gave way to businesses and restaurants as he drew nearer to the center of town. A feeling of misery grew inside him. He was tired; he had stayed up too late underneath his covers with a flashlight greedily reading his favorite books.

Books where adventurers rebelled against alien dictatorships on strange planets and bravely fought against forces of evil with laser guns and laser swords. In those books, the villains were the greedy people who made innocent children work against their will. In those books, the villain was defeated, order restored, justice victorious.

He made it to the detasseling pickup point where a spattering of other kids were seated, strewed around grass alongside the road. All of them were wearing a similar outfit to Ralph: shorts with long socks and long-sleeve shirts, despite the heat, to avoid injury while out in the rough and tearing cornfield. He could tell by the thin number that he'd arrived early, and inwardly he kicked himself for not allowing himself a few extra minutes of precious sleep.

He recognized Billy, a kid he was vaguely familiar with from school, seated on the curb. Ralph set his bike alongside the others on a rack and sat down next to him.

"Hi," said Ralph.

Billy turned towards him. "You want to see something cool?"

"Sure."

He reached into his pocket, dug around, and produced a pack of cigarettes.

"I swiped them from my stepdad," Billy said. He flipped the lid open. "You want to try one?"

For a moment, Ralph considered it. He could show his father that he wasn't keeping him away from the "bad kids." He sent him directly towards them.

Ralph got nauseous, however, while considering this. He knew that cigarettes were a symbol of something that he was not. He shook his head.

"Your loss," said Billy. "They're awesome."

He stood and walked towards an alleyway that led behind the store-fronts across the street.

Ralph sat there for what felt like forever, watched the sun rise higher into the sky, felt the rising heat that he knew would only get worse as the day progressed. More kids arrived at the pickup stop. Billy came back, reeking of smoke.

A school bus squealed to a slow stop in front of the group of thirty-or-so kids. They piled in.

Only ten kids were dropped off at the site alongside the country road where Ralph would work until three o'clock. It was a smaller farm than what the detasseling service typically dealt with. The bus driver had explained to the kids on their first day that the family who owned the farm, the Snyders, had typically dealt with their own detasseling. This year, however, they'd decided they needed extra hands for the task.

Billy and Ralph stood alongside the rest of the kids in their crew as they all pulled on their heavy, damp gloves and set their netted hats over their faces. Ralph felt sick to his stomach knowing what he'd have to endure for the next seven hours.

The bus driver had dropped them off directly in front of the corn fields. The lone house on the property, a shabby, crooked one-story home stood far down the road.

"You all know what areas you're responsible for?" the bus driver hollered from the driver's seat.

All ten kids, standing on a barren stretch of country road with no adult supervision, nodded glumly.

"Great. Don't bother the farmers. Don't be loud. I'll be back at three."

And with that, the doors on the bus closed and it pulled away.

Ralph trudged to his section of field, which was furthest from where they were dropped off. It ran against a patch of woods that extended down the length of the corn.

Immediately his shoes and long socks were soaked through. They absorbed the dew and moisture from the dirt like sponges. Detasseling consisted of grabbing the top of a corn plant firmly and pulling up, removing the stamen from the rest of the plant. Mentally, he overlaid the faces of anyone who'd ever hurt him or made him angry across the fronts of the stamens: he imagined he was throttling their throats and popping off their heads.

The sun beat down on Ralph from directly overhead. He'd rolled his socks down to try and beat some of the unbearable heat. His water bottle was empty, and he'd barely finished two of the rows of corn. His hands felt raw underneath his gloves, his eyes stung from sweat dripping into them.

"*OW!*"

Something snagged his leg. Ralph felt the white searing heat of flesh being ripped open. He looked down, and blood was pouring out of a wound in his leg. He stumbled off past the row of corn he'd already detasseled towards the shaded woods.

Immediately, the thick treetops overhead blocked out the oppressive heat. He took in the coolness as he searched for a comfortable place to sit and treat his wound. He watched the blood begin to pool around his bunched-up sock and absorb into it. He felt woozy at the sight, or he felt woozy with dehydration and exhaustion, or perhaps it was a mix of both.

The further he got from the sunlight behind him the cooler he felt, so he stumbled on, stepping over snarled bushes and downed branches.

Ralph stopped. On the trunk of a tree, ten feet in front of him, was a blood-red painting of a strange star. He looked around. There were more like it on trees further into the woods. Ralph's mind went to the stories he read in his bed at night—stories of visitors from the stars, of UFOs, of alien abductions. He shuddered, a mixture of nervousness and excitement churning in his stomach.

The paintings on the trees grew more frequent and more grotesque the further Ralph walked. Agonized faces were depicted as well as beings rising from the ground. Rotting ears of corn were attached to some. And then he found himself in a clearing. His breathing and heartbeat quickened as he took in what was before him.

Two rows of hazardous benches were set towards the center of the clearing. They faced towards a thin cross. Something had been ripped from the cross where the two pieces of wood were attached to each other. Yellowed shards jutted from the wood. They looked like filed-down teeth.

He looked around, to see if whoever—or *what*ever—was responsible for building this perverse approximation of Sunday Service lurked nearby. But no, Ralph was alone. The only sounds he could hear were the rhythmic pumping of his heart and that of nature's—trees rustling in the stale summer air, insects chirping across the dry dirt floor.

Ralph approached the cross and reached out his arm to touch it. He pulled back when his foot squished into something soft and moist. He looked down. Some of the dirt on the ground had been stained and dampened by something—something red.

Ralph leapt away, the sound of his heart now drowning out any other noise around him. He smashed into one of the benches behind him, fell onto the seat. He heard the wood crack and wheeze underneath his weight. He stared at the pool of red underneath the cross, wild-eyed, clutching the bench.

He took deep breaths to calm himself. His eyes focused on the trees at the far edge of the clearing, focused on the red paintings upon them. He looked back at the pool that he'd been standing in. "Paint," he said aloud. "It's paint."

Ralph laughed at himself, halfheartedly. He lifted his wounded leg, which had mostly stopped bleeding, took off his sock, and wrapped it around the gash. Then he stood and briskly walked back in the direction from which he came.

He emerged from the corn into the area where the bus had dropped them off that morning. A young man was standing by the road with his back to Ralph. He was combing his long, unkempt hair back with his fingers. When he heard Ralph approaching, he swung around. His eyes were rimmed with dark bags. He was gaunt and almost vibrated with nervousness.

"Hello," he said in a stilted, sing-song voice.

"Hi," said Ralph.

"You're bleeding," said the man, wide-eyed. He pointed to Ralph's makeshift bandage, which was soaked through with red. His eyes narrowed. "Look, my parents can't afford to pay if you're planning on suing. You can sue, but you can't tap a dry well. You just can't."

"I just... the corn." Ralph pointed behind himself sheepishly. "I'm not gonna..."

"Oh, I'm just messing around," the man said and forced a laugh. "Do you need anything?"

"I think it's mostly stopped."

Ralph still felt dazed by his discovery in the woods. He wanted to ask the man if he knew anything about it, but he didn't want to get in trouble for leaving his post for as long as he had.

The man grunted, then turned back towards the road. "What time does this guy come to pick you kids up?"

"Three," said Ralph.

The man checked his watch. "Not long. One of the other kids, um, Bobby, or something..."

"Billy?" Ralph offered.

"Right. Billy. His mom came to pick him up. Family emergency... or something."

"Oh." Ralph felt a tinge of disappointment. He had been excited to tell Billy about what he'd seen at the clearing in the woods. He knew that he'd be interested in that sort of thing.

"Yeah, and I probably need to let this guy know," said the man. He scratched at his face and turned back towards Ralph. Then, his eyes lit up. "Do you think you could tell him for me?"

"Me?"

"Yeah. I just, I have stuff I should be doing. Important stuff. Would you do that for me? Tell the guy?"

Ralph shrugged. "Yeah, I can do that."

"Awesome. Thank you," the man said, nodding, wide-eyed. "Really. Thank you." Then he turned and walked off towards the shabby house in the distance.

When the bus arrived, nine kids piled on. Ralph stepped in last. "Hey. Billy had to get picked up early. There was a family emergency."

"Billy?"

"Yeah, he's one of the—"

"Just go sit down."

Ralph shrugged, and walked to the back of the bus.

At dinner that night, his father asked how work was. Ralph chewed on his bottom lip.

"I think there might be aliens out there," he said.

His father nearly spat his beer onto the table. "Mexicans?"

"What?"

"You said—"

"He doesn't mean aliens like *that* honey," said Ralph's mom, turning her face so she could roll her eyes in secret.

"You mean make believe aliens?" his father shouted. "Like those aliens in those sissy comic books you read?"

Ralph stared at his father. "I just saw some weird...,"

"I sent you out there this summer so you could learn to be a man. I don't want to hear another word about comic books and make believe come out of your mouth ever again."

"Somebody offered me a cigarette today," Ralph blurted out. Silence settled over the table.

"Who?" his dad asked through clenched teeth.

"You didn't take it, honey.... Right?" his mom asked, breathless.

"No, I didn't take it."

"Who?" his father shouted.

"A kid named Billy," said Ralph. He immediately regretted telling them about it.

"Stay away from him," said his father. He took a sip of his beer. "And you are going back there to work. No matter what alien or cigarette bullshit you pitch at my dinner table."

Later that night, while the family sat in front of the television, there was a knock on their door. Ralph's mom looked towards the clock ticking above them. "Who could that be?"

Ralph's father struggled to get out of his chair. He stood, bleary-eyed, and mumbled, "I'll get it."

Ralph heard the door open and the faint sounds of a woman speaking. After about a minute, he heard, "Ralph!" barked from the front door. Ralph stood and walked to the front room.

A woman stood underneath his father's looming presence. "This is that Billy boy's mother," his father slurred. "D'you know where he is?"

"I haven't seen him all day, not since this morning when he left to detassel," the woman said. She sounded frantic and breathless. "I've been calling around to the other parents, but everyone I've asked has said their kids were at the McCoy farm today. Do you—did you see him?"

"Yeah. He was at work. I thought... he said that you came to pick him up."

"Billy said that?"

Dread filled Ralph's stomach. A lump formed in his throat. "No, he... he... the guy. One of the farmers. At the place where we were working. He said that, he said... you came to pick up Billy."

The woman's face contorted in distress. Ralph's father was not fazed.

"Look lady," he said. "From what I heard, your son's one of the bad ones. The way I see it, he cut out early because he doesn't understand the value of a hard day's work, and now he's holed up with whatever hooligans smoking *God knows what*. Now, if you don't mind, I'm trying to have family time. *My* son doesn't know anything about *your* delinquent."

Just before the door slammed shut, Ralph glimpsed Billy's mother. He could see the dread that he felt reflected ten-fold in her eyes.

The next day, Ralph rode his bicycle to the town's center as quickly as he could. He hoped that Billy would already be sitting there by the time he arrived. Any thoughts of grueling heat and corn detasseling were gone. He just wanted to see Billy so that the visions of the shrine he'd found in the woods would dull. He wanted to know for certain that the red puddle he'd stepped in the day before was simply red paint.

When he arrived at the bus pickup point, however, there was no Billy. In fact, in his haste, Ralph was the first to arrive there. He tucked his bike into a nearby rack, sat, and waited.

As minutes ticked by, children glumly strolled and biked up to the spot. None of them were Billy. Still, Ralph gazed longingly at each one, hoping he'd arrive.

And then the bus squealed to a halt on the road in front of him. Ralph could feel his heart attempting to escape his chest through his mouth. He stepped onto the bus, and stopped.

The driver turned to look. "What's the hold up?"

"Is there any news?" asked Ralph.

"*What?*"

"Is there any news. About Billy?"

"Billy?"

"I... nevermind."

"Go sit down, we have places to be."

When Ralph took a seat toward the back of the bus, his head was spinning. Everybody was acting as if everything was normal. And now, the reality that he'd be going back to that farm, back to that shrine, set in.

The bus rumbled to a stop. Ralph had been clenching his eyes shut for most of the drive, attempting to regulate his bodily functions. His heartrate, his breathing.

"You're all gonna be getting out here!" the bus driver shouted from the front. "At the McCoy farm."

Ralph pressed his face to the window and saw a massive piece of land spread out before him. A state-of-the-art tractor sat alongside the sprawling fields of corn. He couldn't see a single patch of forest anywhere. Relief and confusion replaced the dread that had been building in him for the entire drive there.

Ralph was the last off the bus.

"Why are we all getting off here?" he asked the driver.

The driver gawked at him. "Are you serious kid? Because... look, I just do what I'm told!" Ralph continued standing there. "Get off the bus!"

Ralph emerged to see all the other kids pulling on their gloves and donning their netted hats. After a moment, he did the same. Everyone acted as if everything was normal.

He detasseled corn until three o'clock. He did so with efficiency, pulling the stamens clear off from the rest of the plant, repeatedly. He'd finished his entire section before quitting time and had barely noticed the oppressive heat or the tiny cuts the plants made on his skin.

That night, there was another knock on the door. "Jesus Christ," Ralph's father muttered as he went to go answer it. After a moment, he heard, "Ralph, could you please come here, son?"

When Ralph arrived at the door, a police officer greeted him from outside. "Hey there, Ralph," the officer said.

"He's here about that Billy," said his father. "He hasn't been found yet."

The police officer nodded. "Ralph, we just wanted to do a little follow up with you about Billy Marston. Nobody's heard from him since yesterday, and his mom said that you seemed like you might have some information for us about his whereabouts."

"Like I said, Officer," his father again spoke. "He's out doing God knows what with God kn...."

"He's on that farm," Ralph interrupted. He could feel his father's eyes boring a hole in the side of his skull. "The one we were detasseling at on Wednesday. We didn't go back there today. He's there."

The officer shook his head. "Yes, that's the last place he was seen. But the Snyders have been very cooperative with our investigation. We already looked around the property and are confident that he is no longer at that farm. What I need from you is—did he say anything? Anything which might've indicated a plan to run away?"

Ralph gaped at the man. He felt hysterical. "Look, there's a freaking—there's like total alien paintings on the trees in the woods—I swear to God he's gotta be...."

His father grabbed the back of Ralph's head and pushed his face into his stomach, stifling the boy's words. "I'm sorry about him, Officer. He's—those comic books. You know what they do to a kid's brain. And he just won't stop reading them."

The police officer nodded in understanding.

"Just between you and me," said his father. "Ralph told me that *Billy* offered him a cigarette the day he went missing. He sounds like a bad, bad seed."

The police officer nodded in understanding.

Ralph was sent to his room with no supper for *talking crazy to the authorities*. He sat there for hours, staring at his bookshelf. His eyes lingered on the books; books filled with brave adventurers who fought for what was right.

When he heard his parents go to bed, Ralph waited fifteen minutes before creeping downstairs. He went to his family's den and slid open a desk drawer, producing a map of Sturgis Falls and the surrounding area. He unfolded it and scanned the area to the east of town until he found what he was looking for.

Snyder Farm

He folded the map back up, stuck it into his backpack, then went to fetch his bike from the garage.

All he could see were dark outlines of trees as he trudged through the woods as quietly as possible. It was slow going, partly due to the hazardous terrain, and partly due to the utter fear coursing through him. His body was slick with sweat from the ride, but any fatigue that it had caused was forgotten due to the adrenaline surging within.

Ralph brought his face close to each tree that he passed, searching for the illustrations that he'd seen the other day.

And then, he froze.

Off in the distance was a flicker. He watched the flame wavering there. It was set upon a torch that was stuck in the ground.

He covered his mouth, got down to the forest floor, and began his slow approach to the flame.

As he got closer, he could hear indistinct male speech overlaid by an even fainter animalistic whining. He stopped when he could make out the form of a cloaked person silhouetted by the fire's light. Ralph could now barely make out the words the man was saying.

"...for you now, to accept this offer would be the grandest of honors. His head will be for you, dear Lord, bestowed here for all to see. His blood will absorb into the ground, and I pray—I *pray*, dear Lord, that you will take that and make it bountiful...."

The flame blew about in the wind, casting the clearing in different lights. Ralph could see the cross, but underneath the cross was a dark shape he did not recognize.

Then the flame blew in the wind and light was cast on the shape and Ralph had to bite down on the back of his hand in order not to scream.

The torch illuminated the face of Billy, who was gagged and seated against the cross. His eyes stared up at the cloaked man in utter distress. He was making the animalistic sounds that Ralph had been hearing; sounds of unimaginable fear.

The cloaked man held in his hand a knife.

If Ralph were a character in one of his books, he would've stood, run towards the man, knocked him over. Punched him, kicked him, stabbed him. He would've done anything at all.

But he didn't.

Instead, he listened to the blood rush in his own ears and watched, frozen, as the robed man lifted his knife, and plunged it into the side of the screaming, thrashing boy's throat.

That's when feeling came back into Ralph's legs. That's when he regained his faculties. He stood. He felt a branch underneath his foot snap. The robed man swiveled around, knocking his hood from his head. Ralph recognized him as the man from the house, the deep bags under his eyes accentuated by the light cast by the flame.

Then, taking one last look at the bleeding, gagged Billy, Ralph took off from the direction he came.

He leapt over branches and navigated the black forest as if he were a lithe bear. As if he'd been born there. He didn't allow any thoughts to dictate his actions. He just ran. From behind him, he could hear the man, bellowing and running after him. There was a high-pitched ringing sounding in Ralph's ears. As he ran, he became aware that this sound was coming from his own mouth. He was screaming.

He emerged from the woods into a cornfield. He ran through the corn, ignoring the scratches, lifting his legs high to avoid tripping. He tore out of the cornfield and found himself staring up at the Snyders' house. His blood froze when he saw that all the lights in the house were on.

"Are you okay?"

He leapt back. Standing a few feet away from him was an old man dressed in pajamas. He held a shotgun across his chest.

Ralph took off running without a word.

The last thing he heard the man say before he got out of earshot was, "Jesus Christ he did it again. Jesus Christ."

The sun was beginning to rise by the time Ralph made it to the sign that read *Welcome to Sturgis Falls*. He had been unable to locate his bike in the dark, so he ran. He used the map folded in his backpack to haphazardly navigate home.

His body was shaking with fatigue and adrenaline as he approached his front door. He was covered in cuts and dried blood. He lifted a shaky fist up to the door and knocked three times.

His mother threw it open a minute later. Her face was pale. "Ralph Hutchinson, where the *hell—*"

She was interrupted by her son falling into her arms, sobbing.

Ralph sat on the edge of his bed with his face in his hands.

He'd brought the police to the Snyder farm, to show them what he'd seen. He'd brought them into the woods, past the trees with stars painted on their trunks. He'd brought them to the clearing. In the clearing, there was nothing. No benches. No cross. No Billy. No red puddle.

The old farmer and his wife stood outside their front door, arms crossed. Ralph recognized the old man, but the old man did not seem to recognize him. "Are you satisfied?" the man asked, speaking only to the police officers, ignoring Ralph and his family.

"We are very sorry, Mr. Snyder," one of the officers said. "If you don't mind me asking, what's the deal with the pentagrams and such painted on all the trees out there?"

"I do mind you asking. But if you really must know, my son. He's troubled. Got into the whole devil worship thing that the youth are into these days. We had to send him away."

"So he's not on the property?" asked the officer.

"No," the old man said curtly. He flashed his eyes to Ralph and then looked back to the officer. "Hasn't been for months."

Ralph wanted to scream. He wanted to sprint into the old man at full speed. He wanted to knock him over.

He didn't do any of that.

Instead, he went home. He went up to his room. He sat on his bed. He put his face in his hands.

It was clear that even his mother, who'd wholeheartedly believed his story that morning, had begun to think that he'd made the whole thing up to get out of detasseling. It was either that, or her son was deeply troubled, and she'd never choose to believe such a thing.

Slowly, he removed his face from his hands. He looked up towards his bookshelf. The myriad books that lined the wood had brought him great comfort and inspiration for as long as he could remember. Now, it was like the color had been sucked out of them. He saw them for what they were. Ink and pulped trees. Nothing more.

From outside he heard children playing in the street. He thought of Billy. The police were looking for him, now. Ralph knew they wouldn't find him. They were looking for him in back alleys, asking locally known troublemakers if they had any ideas where the kid had gone. Ralph knew they wouldn't find him. Ralph knew that they were looking in the wrong places, that to find Billy the police would have to cross the city limits. They'd have to cross the cornfield. They'd have to go into the woods.

But nobody would listen to Ralph. Nobody would believe him. Evil occurred in the cities and towns where idleness was left to fester and become something rotten. Nothing bad ever happened out there in the fields, where hardworking people do hard work while thinking of only moral things, like corn.

***

About the Author

Cole Thorna was born and raised in Upstate New York. He decided to move to the cornfields of Iowa in July of 2019. Since then he's cooked countless hamburgers, learned how to drive, and, most recently, enrolled at University of Iowa where he is studying English and Creative Writing.

9

NO TOE

By Edward Narigon

It was a time of social change in Southwest Iowa in the 1950s. As times got tough the family farms—farmed and lived in by a single family—were disappearing, absorbed by prosperous neighbors and investors. As this continued the landscape gradually changed. As you drove down the hilly, gravel roads you noticed two or three ramshackle farmhouses in every mile. Once the sole house on a plot of farmland, they were now occupied by hired men and their families working for the larger farms. Occasionally you would drive by a newer, modern farmhouse surrounded by painted fences with nice gravel driveways and mowed lawns. This is where the landowners lived.

I attended a rural school that consisted of four classrooms, a small gymnasium and, a half-acre of nice yard with some playground equipment. In my grade there were nine kids, and we were occasionally split up between two classrooms. Four of us would attend class with the next upper grade level and the other five would attend with the lower grade level. The teachers would share their time with both grade levels.

As a farm kid, your friends were whoever lived closest to you. Nobody cared about the clothes you wore. Whether they were bought new at the town store or whether your mom sewed patches in the knees of your jeans. No matter which house you lived in, the shack or the stately farmhouse with the white picket fence, we all played cowboys and Indians in the woods or had war games with discarded corn cobs.

Looking back, I now realize that a significant number of students at our little schoolhouse were living in poverty. In third grade there was a student named Marvin who seldom brought lunch from home. While the rest of us would gather our lunch boxes and pull out our peanut butter and jelly sandwiches and sticks of carrots, Marvin would sit at his desk and just stay quiet.

The young ladies in the class decided to bring items for his lunch and the first day they presented Marvin with his own brown lunch sack with the sandwich and an apple he didn't know how to react. He was never the center of attention and that day when he got his sack lunch his face turned red, and he put his head down in his arms on his desk and wept. But he ate it.

My family lived in a rented house at the top of a hill on a gravel road. The countryside was a mix of crops, pasture, and dense woods with the Nishnabotna River winding through the timber that filled each valley. The landlord lived next to us and had a nice newer house. Our house was decent, but old-fashioned. There was no central heating so the furnace would heat up the basement and then there were vents in the floors for the heat to rise through the house.

Down the gravel road a half mile there was an old farmhouse, probably built in the 19th century. The peeling sideboards were unpainted. Some of the windows were boarded up. The dirt driveway was littered with rusted up farm implements from long ago. The yard was overgrown with neglected grass, weeds and unkempt shrubbery. The front porch was crooked and missing some planks.

Raymond and his sister Jenny lived there with their parents. The father, whose family lost their farmland down in Missouri during the Great Depression, was a hired man for our landlord. In the summer he worked from sunup to sundown tilling soil for the crops, moving cattle from one field to the next, and such. In winter he kept the livestock fed and manure slopped.

Raymond was a couple of years younger than me—about the same age as my brother. Raymond wore ragged bib overalls that were too large for him so the pants were rolled up several times and his skin and underwear showed through some of the tears. He wore no shirt. I also never saw him wear shoes. He did not attend school.

Jenny was about six years old and had white, blonde hair that hung to the middle of her back. She always had on a blue cotton dress that my mom said was made from an old flour sack. She also lacked shoes; and her feet and ankles were dark brown with the dust from her yard and driveway. We seldom saw her outside.

My brother and I spent time playing with Raymond in the timber and pastures around our houses. We explored the trails in the woods that led to the river and made forts in heavy brush piles by downed trees. We spent hours making tree houses and fished in the river and small ponds with poles made from willow branches and worms and grasshoppers for bait. We learned to make snares and use spring traps to catch rabbits and used my Dad's single-shot .410 shotgun to hunt squirrels and birds.

Our prize kill was a pheasant I shot out of the air. It was autumn and the chill—and Mom—forced us to wear our wool flannel overcoats. Raymond wore a repurposed feed sack stuffed with cotton. We laid out there on the near frozen ground of a harvested field, the brown cornstalks flattened to the earth. I had that shotgun poised at the ready. Raymond huddled between my brother and I, shivering. Our American shepherd mix, Bailey, rustled up some pheasants and two of them took flight. With dumb luck—I'm pretty sure both my eyes were closed—I hit one of the birds just right and it fell right out of the air. I knew Mom wouldn't be too happy we were playing with guns out in the landowner's cornfield so I gave the bird to Raymond. He was pleased as punch.

Looking back with the experience of an adult I realized now that Raymond and Jenny were severely undernourished and mistreated. Raymond always seemed to have bruises on his arms and sometimes on his face. Jenny occasionally had red stripes on her legs. At the time I just ignored that but now I realize that it was probably from beatings received from her parents. I am now amazed as kids that we could look past such signs of abuse.

So we played happily with our neighbors, mostly Raymond, but every once in a while, Jenny played if we were in their yard. Jenny liked to catch snails and bugs, especially the roly polys. Occasionally we could see their mother watching us through a window, but she never came outside.

It was near winter, and the temperature took a nosedive. The heat rising from below felt good coming to the registers in our bedroom. One morning I went out to do my chores to feed and water our small herd of pigs. We had three sows, and they were having their litters of pigs. I planned to show these litters at the annual 4-H fair next summer.

On this morning as I entered the shed a dark figure rose up from the stack of straw bales. It was Raymond. He was shivering and wearing only his ragged overalls. In the dim light, his pallid skin and blonde hair along with his large dark eyes made him appear ghostly. He was trembling.

"What are you doing here?" I asked.

"Hiding" said Raymond. Tears were welling in his eyes and starting to spill down his dusty cheeks. I didn't know what to say. I took off my flannel jacket and handed it to him.

Back at the kitchen, I told Mom what I had found. "What do you mean Raymond is in the shed?'

"He said he is hiding," I said.

"Well, bring him up here and let's see what is going on…"

At the shed, I told Raymond to come with me to the house. He groaned as he struggled to get up, and as he swung his leg over the short fence, I saw a cloth feed sack wound around his foot. It was drenched in blood. Raymond hobbled over to me without putting any weight on his foot. With his arm over my shoulder, we went to the kitchen.

Once inside, in my mom's scrubbed kitchen, I became aware of the scent of unwashed clothes, and body, and the acrid smell of blood. Mom sat at a chair adjoining Raymond and lifted the bandaged foot to her lap. Carefully, she unwrapped the feed sack, and gasped as she uncovered the wound.

"Why, your little toe is gone! What happened?"

I peeked and immediately wished I hadn't. Where his pinky toe had been there was now a gory wound with a bone sticking out. His entire foot was covered in partially congealed blood with clots and pieces of straw. I felt like urping but fought the urge.

There was no 911 then. And no phone at Raymond's house. My Mom called the research farm where Dad worked and told the receptionist to have him call home. Thirty minutes later he called, and once he heard the story, he drove quickly home. We waited, and Raymond drifted in and out of consciousness, his foot now wrapped in old rags my mom kept under the sink in case of spills.

Once home, Dad looked at Raymond's wound and told Mom to call the police and an ambulance. He looked at me and said, "Let's go."

We drove the white Chevy work pickup down the road to Raymond's house, kicking up gravel and dust as we went, fishtailing through the loose gravel. Dad pulled into the dirt driveway and parked in front of the house. The front door was open, and we walked up the crooked steps and into the house. There was blood spattered on the floor of the kitchen. Raymond's mom was sprawled on the floor, arms outstretched as if she were only napping. Her face was a shade of pale blue. There were purple bruises around her throat and a bloody gash on her forehead. It was the longest I ever looked at her face.

Dad turned her over and felt for a pulse. He went into the next room, a bedroom, and said, "Don't come in here. Get in the truck."

I turned to go, and as I did, I heard a thumping sound. I saw a trunk by the kitchen wall. The top was closed. A latch was held by a bent nail, but it allowed a gap. I saw two white fingers sticking out through the gap. I pulled out the nail and opened the lid. Jenny, her long silky hair a tangled mess, struggled to sit up. I helped her out and holding hands, we ran to the pickup, which was still idling in the driveway.

A minute later, Dad came out to the truck. We drove back to our house, Jenny sitting between us like a porcelain doll. Dad was silent.

As we arrived at our driveway, a sheriff's patrol car cruised up the hill and pulled into our drive. Dad, Jenny, and I went into the kitchen, followed shortly by the deputy. Within twenty minutes we had four law enforcement vehicles, red lights flashing, crowded around our house. They all just got in each other's way.

I went to the back porch, where three officers were standing, one flicking the ashes from his cigarette on my mom's flowers.

"Never seen anything like it..." said one. "He'd been stabbed and stabbed."

"And Howard said he found a toe ..."

Raymond never spoke to anyone after that day. A childless couple took him in, but after a year he ran away. Jenny entered the childcare system, and I only saw her occasionally from a distance. She was beautiful.

A year later, I went in to the hog shed to do my morning chores, and a figure rose up from the straw pile. Raymond looked at me and then nodded his head. He reached over and handed me two fresh-killed pheasants. I asked him what he was doing, where he lived ... but he just looked at me. I gave him my coat and mittens. Then he walked away, around the corner of the shed, and towards the timber.

I always wondered what happened to him. But that day he left me, I noticed he was barefoot, and he left footprints in the soft ground. And one footprint was missing the little toe.

The story isn't over... tales of a ghost in the woods, or "tramps'" starting campfires along the river, and missing lumber from the scrap piles, keep the story alive. And every once in a while, in the early morning, I'll find a fresh pheasant, or a couple of rabbits or squirrels, freshly dressed, on top of the straw stack in the hog shed. And if there is soft ground, I might find a footprint... missing a little toe. And every fall, I leave a coat on the straw.

***

About the Author

Edward J. Narigon grew up in rural communities of Southwest Iowa and learned to work by raising livestock, walking beans, detasseling corn, and gathering hay bales for family members and neighboring farmers. After a few years working in hog production, he started a lengthy career with Farm Credit Services of America providing agricultural loans and financial services to agricultural producers in Iowa, Nebraska, South Dakota and Wyoming. He volunteered his time to Boy Scouts of America as a troop leader, district leader and council leader. Following his interest in martial arts, he earned a 3rd Degree Black Belt in Seishin Ryu Karate and served as arbitrator for tournaments. Now successfully retired, he spends time with his friends and family, camping, and numerous hobbies.

10

GUESTS IN THE PARLOR

BY JENNY FEE

"**Y**ou go on if you want to. I wouldn't cross that fence if my life depended on it."

I paused, one hand still gripping the steel post, the other resting on the sagging woven wire beside it. Was Maggie right? I glanced over my shoulder at my sister, three years my senior but lifetimes smarter. If you asked her.

"I thought college would've made you fun," I grumbled, stepping back but still eyeing the old Whitaker place. "Don't you want to do anything exciting this summer?"

The ancient farmhouse towered just twenty yards ahead of us, white paint peeling, roof sagging. It was so nearly hidden beneath vines and straggly trees that it seemed more like a fixture of the land—another knoll or thicket—than the handiwork of an Iowa pioneer.

"I can think of better things than to have an old house fall in on me," Maggie retorted. "Besides, I thought you were scared of this place. Didn't somebody die here or something?"

I groaned. Leave it to her to be so nonchalant about a century-old murder mystery practically in our backyard. And, yes, the house terrified me just as much as when we were kids. I remembered those recurring nightmares.

The only difference now was that curiosity was getting the better of me. Lily Whitaker had come home on a summer's afternoon in 1925 to find her parents and little brother bludgeoned to death by an axe. The case had never been solved—unless you counted the rumors that teenage Lily had done it herself.

"I'm walking home," Maggie announced, jolting me from my reverie. I nearly trailed after her—childhood habits die hard – but stayed rooted in my spot as she disappeared around the bend. The lane to our own farmhouse was just out of sight.

I leaned on the fence again, inhaling deeply as though to breathe in courage. I would just peek through a window—one window—to see what was inside.

Just then the shrill of cicadas seemed to escalate to a roar. The sultry calm of the day swirled into a gusty wind, causing the old house to groan and shaking the leaves of the gnarled oaks surrounding it.

And what was that other sound? An old-fashioned song, tinny as though drifting from a radio or Victrola...

Just like a melody that lingers on
You seem to haunt me night and day
I never realized till you had gone
   How much I cared about you...

Then, silence.

Ignoring the shaking of my hands, I hoisted myself over the fence, the wire scraping at my legs already a map of mosquito bites and poison ivy rashes. *The marks of a good summer,* my grandma always teased me. She'd been an explorer like me in her younger years, growing up on the same Century Farm where my family lived now.

Still, I tiptoed through the overgrown front yard as though it were dotted with land mines. There was no sense waking the dead. And if my parents happened to drive by, I'd never hear the end of it.

I stepped onto the porch, expecting the wooden floorboards to creak under foot. Instead, they gave a little with each step, rot making them spongy and quiet. Next to the front door was a diamond-shaped window not much bigger than my face, gray with dust in the middle but surrounded by brilliant squares of stained glass.

Had that been Mrs. Whitaker's pride and joy in her otherwise-plain farmhouse? I used the palm of my hand to try to wipe it off and leaned in, prepared to see a room in shambles.

Instead, I spied a kitchen table set for three, a vase of shriveled wildflowers in the middle. Behind it, an enamel coffee pot still sat on a cast iron stove. It was a hazy scene through the leaded glass, but it looked as though, aside from the layer of dust on everything, the house's owner might start cooking supper any minute.

Supper! As if on cue, I caught a whiff of bacon, onions, and potatoes frying. Homemade bread fresh from the oven. When had Mom ever made that before?

I carefully backtracked away from the house, then practically hurdled the fence to run all the way home. The last thing I wanted was for my parents to ask me why I'd been late.

I wouldn't lie to them if they did, just as I knew Maggie wouldn't tattle on me—the Davis family code of honor. But she did look smug as I pushed lettuce around my plate a few minutes later.

"Something wrong, Kat?" our mom asked. "I thought you liked chef salad."

"I do," I said, despite the roiling in my stomach. "Just thought we were having something different. Must've imagined it."

***

The next morning, I made a beeline down a familiar hallway at Shady Grove Assisted Living. I knew by heart where to turn into Grandma's room, but even if I didn't, her door was unmistakable. It was covered with cut-out pictures of leading men from the Golden Age of Hollywood, especially Kirk Douglas in tight swimming shorts.

"Grams?" I called out, pushing her door ajar just wide enough for me to step inside. As I always did, I plucked a butterscotch from her candy dish and plopped down on her bed.

"Kat!" she exclaimed as soon as she came to from her nap in her recliner, beaming as though she hadn't just seen me a couple days earlier. "What brings you by?"

"I need you to tell me something," I replied without hesitation. "What happened at the Whitaker place?"

Her lined face went from beaming to befuddled in an instant. "Why on earth would you ask that? Better to stay far, far away and not even talk about it. I wish some fire bug would've burned it down years ago."

I weighed my words, mindful that Grandma was 90 years old and had a bad heart. "But, Grandma, I can't help seeing it. It's right next door. Besides," I blurted out, "I went there yesterday."

"Child, child," she said. The words might as well have been "tsk, tsk." She studied me for a long moment, then hobbled across the room to her dresser, rummaging through a drawer until she held an envelope in her wrinkled hands.

"I don't even know why I kept it," she murmured, holding it out to me. "But I'm glad now that I did. Maybe if you know the truth, you'll realize it's no place for you to go poking around."

Inside was a single, yellowed newspaper clipping with a black-and-white photo of a girl about my age. She had bobbed hair set in waves and big, solemn eyes. Her silky blouse had a bow at the collar, pearl buttons, and a pattern that looked like row after row of wilted single tulips.

"Lily Whitaker in happier days," the caption beneath read, "now the lone survivor of Saturday's brutal slayings."

I gulped, then scanned the article beneath. Lily had come home late in the afternoon after driving the family's Model T to town for an ice cream social. Found a bloody axe lying in the front yard. The front door wide open. Bodies in the parlor.

There were no suspects, as "the late Mr. and Mrs. Whitaker had no enemies. This was surely a case of a deranged transient passing through by way of boxcar," the article had decreed. "Left to mourn is the lovely Lily Whitaker, age 17, who we suppose will soon marry or move to other parts unshrouded by the dark cloud of this tragedy."

I blinked, checking the envelope for any more clippings.

"That's it?" I asked Grandma. "I know it was never solved. But it wasn't written about again? Half of this isn't even facts—just flowery talk. What did Lily do afterward?"

Grandma shot me a pained look, digging a tissue out of her pocket to wipe her nose. "Well, she didn't do much," she replied. "She stayed in that house the rest of her life. They say she was seen at church early on—sometimes showed up at a bridal shower or sewing bee. But by the time I was a little girl—that would've been twenty years later—she mostly kept to herself. When her car quit running, she'd walk to town if she ever needed to go to the store.

"People would stare at her, see," Grandma continued. "Whisper when they thought she wasn't paying attention. Half of the town thought Lily had done it. But even if you didn't, best just to stay away."

I realized my mouth was hanging open. It wasn't at all the story I'd expected. First Lily found her family murdered. Then the community sentenced her to life in exile?

"But, Grandma, your family lived next door," I said. "Your parents checked on her, right?"

"A couple times, Daddy pulled the car over when we passed her walking to town. But Lily wouldn't climb in, no matter how hot or cold it was," Grandma murmured, looking past me to the wall—to the memory. "Said she was sure her parents would be along shortly and didn't want to worry them."

A chill ran down my spine. I could imagine my great-grandfather at the wheel of his beloved Ford pickup with a pint-sized Grandma and all her siblings piled in the back, peeking over the top of the wood sideboards.

I envisioned the girl in the newspaper clipping—now with gray streaking her hair and a few more pounds on her frame—leaning toward the unrolled window. *Thank you all the same for asking, Mr. Davis. I'll tell Mama and Daddy that they missed you.* Then the truck slowly driving away, leaving Lily in a haze of dust to trod on.

"Lily managed just fine," Grandma added, her jaw taking on a stubborn set. She fumbled with the remote control as though finding "Wheel of Fortune" was suddenly an urgent matter. "She managed just fine till she was older than me even. She died in that house."

***

The nightmare came back that night, playing out just as it had when I was little.

The Whitaker house is bright white again, the vines and snarl of straggly trees gone. Only young oak trees and little flower beds dot the yard, and cheery puffs of gray smoke drift from the chimney.

On the porch, beneath the diamond-shaped window, a little boy in a blue romper sits hunched over a top, cackling as it spins and tips over, again and again. The chubby rolls on his legs wiggle in unison with his belly laughter.

But then the locusts shrill and the wind blows, harder and harder, two forces in bitter competition.

Soon the boy's laughter can't be heard at all. The top won't stay upright to spin even one more time. His angelic face screws itself into a rage, bright red and tear-streaked. His howls join nature's roar.

And then—another noise. The sound of someone chopping wood. Oh, why is someone chopping wood inside? Someone could get hurt....

A woman screams. Suddenly the boy disappears, his top left idle beneath the fancy window. In his place, vines grow with unnatural speed, overtaking an old farmhouse with curling paint and a chimney long gone cold.

***

"It was just a dream," Maggie assured me, squinting as her eyes adjusted to the overhead light being flipped on at 2:36 in the morning.

"I know," I said, pushing sweaty hair out of my face. "But it was the same dream I had a hundred times when we were kids. Isn't it weird it came back?"

"Not really," she said, crossing the bedroom that we still shared when she came home on breaks. She crawled into bed with me, slinging an arm around my shoulders. "When you looked it that window today, you probably just freaked out your subconscious. I learned about it in psychology class."

Sometimes I was thankful that prim and proper Maggie acted more like a second mother than a sister. This was one of those times.

"You're probably right.... You *are* right," I replied, sounding more resolute than I felt. "But I told you what Grandma said. Nobody ever tried to help Lily. What if I'm supposed to go back to that house and—I don't know—do something?"

Maggie sighed but said nothing right away. On the wall in front of us, her collection of trophies and banners for everything from showing pigs at the fair to winning the state track meet, gleamed on a high shelf.

My shelf just beneath was painfully bare, except for a photo of us sitting on the beach at Lake Red Rock, silvery water and red cliffs behind us. I'd been in middle school at the time, she just a couple of grades ahead of me, braces gleaming from both our smiles. Maggie's arm was hanging over my shoulder much as it did now.

"If I go with you," she said after a long while, "we tell no one—and I mean *no one*. And if Mom and Dad find out, you're taking the fall. Deal?"

"Deal."

***

After chores the next morning, Maggie and I set off for the Whitaker place, walking in nervous silence.

Somewhere cows were bellowing for their calves that were probably newly weaned—a mournful chorus. Gravel crunched beneath our sneakers, and wind fluttered the leaves of cottonwood trees along the ditch, imitating the sound of rain.

I had a flashlight wedged into the back pocket of my shorts, hidden beneath my billowy Iowa State T-shirt. Maggie had a screwdriver and bobby pins in hers.

We paused when we came to the fence. Maggie started toward the metal-and-wire gate wide enough for a tractor to pass through. It was only chained shut—not locked. But I shook my head when we made eye contact. If we opened it, it would push the grass down behind it, a dead giveaway for at least a day or two that someone had been here.

I shook my head again as I hoisted myself over the fence. *Who was I becoming?* A criminal. That's who. We'd officially premeditated breaking and entering.

I waited for Maggie, who may have been the better athlete but hadn't scaled nearly as many fences over the years. We waded through the overgrown front yard, a jungle of switchgrass, thistle, and Queen Anne's Lace.

Once in a while, we'd pass a cluster of tall purple phlox or pale pink surprise lilies, remnants of old Mrs. Whitaker's flower beds. Peaches hung rotting on their branches in the fruit orchard just beyond the house. I could smell their sickly-sweetness and see clouds of flies and bees buzzing around.

How ironic, I thought, that these flowers went on blooming and trees kept producing long after the people of the land had faded away.

We stepped onto the porch, and I braced myself for an encore of rushing wind, roaring cicadas, and that eerie Irving Berlin song. Nothing.

"Last chance to go back," Maggie said, her hand poised to try the rusty doorknob. It turned without effort, but she had to push her shoulder against the door to edge it open. It was swollen with humidity and dragged against the uneven floor.

The hazy glow of early morning light filled the kitchen. Maggie gasped when she saw the three place settings ready at the table, the brown flower arrangement in the center. On the Hoosier on the opposite wall, a small crock bowl sat on the counter next to a dusty spoon and glass jar of canned peach slices.

"I don't understand," Maggie said. "It's like she was getting ready to cook and then just left."

I was quiet for a minute, my eyes growing wide in realization.

"Grams said that Lily became an outcast—lived here alone," I explained. "But she must've kept hoping someone would visit, right up until the day she died. Why else would she set the table for three?"

We went into the parlor, careful to tread lightly. The crumbling of the house was more noticeable from inside. Sunshine filtered in through cracks in the walls and the corners of the rooms, and the ceiling had collapsed in places, leaving piles of plaster on the floor and glimpses into the attic.

It was a small room with floor-to-ceiling windows draped in gauzy white curtains. A green velvet settee and rocking chair flanked a wooden cabinet that housed an old-time radio.

The hair raised on the back of my neck as I realized I could hear singing—so hushed that it was nearly undetectable—drifting from within:

Just like a melody that lingers on
You seem to haunt me night and day ...

I knew that Maggie heard it, too, when her screwdriver clattered to the floor and she looked at me, frozen. She'd been holding the tool in front of her as though a weapon.

"*Kat!*" she hissed through a whisper. "You didn't tell me it was haunted. It's actually *haunted*!"

"We don't know that," I replied. I spoke in my regular voice in an effort to show that I wasn't afraid, but it sounded completely out of place, like I was holding a full-volume conversation in the middle of church.

"Maybe someone else has been here, sneaking around," I offered by way of explanation. "Maybe they left the radio on, but it comes in and out so we didn't hear it at first. I'll just turn it off...."

I grabbed the pretty crystal knob of the drop-down door on the lower part of the cabinet. Just then, the gauzy curtains on each of the windows floated outward as though blown by a breeze. Had they been? The windows were shut, but plenty of air could make it through the jagged cracks in the walls.

Glancing out the pane closest to me, I saw that the boughs of the oak trees hung limp, even the leaves unmoving.

Panic rising in my throat, I yanked the door open, desperate to make the music stop. Was I imagining its crescendo? Maggie backed away, slowly shaking her head in horror.

A toy top crashed to the floor, rolling until it reached her feet. She screamed, running through the kitchen and stopping on the front porch.

"Kat!" she wailed. "Kat, come on!"

The top. The same one from my nightmare. But speckled and smudged with burgundy. It continued to spin, round and round, in time with the music. An unholy metronome.

I needed to make it stop. To think. *What's the explanation? Who's crying?* The entire room began to spin like the top. To grow blurry, as though shrouded by a vast gauzy curtain.

I snatched a rag from inside the radio cabinet, intending to grab the toy with it, but dropped it on the floor instead. Not a rag. A blouse. Silky with a pattern of wilted tulips and more haphazard burgundy stains. Hidden away for a century.

I stumbled through the parlor, then the kitchen, to race after Maggie. But not before I saw the flowers in the vase.

Purple phlox, a few thistle blooms and surprise lilies, vibrant as though just now plucked from the earth for guests in the parlor.

***

About the Author

Jenny Fee works as an award-winning journalist, seventh-generation Iowa farmer and volunteer publicist for a bustling cat rescue. She lives with her husband on a historic 1855 farm that they restored from near ruin with the help of family. She's sure it's not haunted – but wisely steers clear of the fruit cellar after dark.

11

DARK MATTER

By Kevin Klingman

He watched the steam rise from his vomit on the concrete steps ascending the church entrance. His clothes were still soaked from trying to drown himself in a cold Des Moines River that November morning. The Entity had denied his attempt. It was still surfacing within him, yet claimed enough ownership to reject such an action. *Why me?* the man thought as he dug in his pocket. His trembling hand pulled out a soggy envelope bleeding with black ink:

Father Hearn

St. Andrew's

550 6th Ave

A din of laughter panned around the man, though no one was in sight. The hallucinations were beginning, the same as they had five years ago. It was getting close. He picked himself up and was plodding toward the massive double doors when the jolt of his recurring headache hit him hard between the eyes. When he unclenched his eyelids, he noticed a small security camera above the doors. He pulled the left door handle and entered.

Once inside, the man was met with the familiar smells of incense, mahogany, must. A faint sound of sheep bleating filled the vestibule and the door locked itself behind him. He took a deep breath and labored toward the holy water fount like he had done at Sacred Heart as a boy and, later, at St. Joseph's when the possessions began. Before his trembling fingers could reach inside the fount, the water turned crimson and overflowed the marble rim. More laughter. More blood, flowing from the eyes of saintly statues, spurting from a wall-mounted crucifix that spun itself counter clockwise several times until it stopped upside down. The Entity was getting stronger by the minute.

As he entered the dark sanctuary, he saw two large objects near the altar, hovering in mid air, encompassed by pillars of dusty light. One was a statue of Mother Mary. The other was the cross, bearing Christ, which had levitated all the way to the arch of the great hall. In the second pew from the front sat a young boy. He looked over his shoulder at the man and pointed his finger at the far left side of the sanctuary. The man looked to see a dark confessional booth that stood ominously against the wall. He kneeled in the aisle, crossed himself, and felt the air shift in front of him. He opened his eyes to see the pews were floating above the floor and facing him. The boy now stood in the middle of the aisle draped in bloodstained linen and encircled by white light.

"He's waiting for you," said the boy. "We've all been waiting for you."

The man rose shakily to his feet and crept behind the pews, his eyes still locked on the altar boy who mirrored the man's gaze through the shadows of his brow. The man arrived at the booth and the door creaked open. His head pulsated to the cadence of his rapid heartbeat. He entered into the darkness. His hand probed around blindly for the seat and when he turned to sit down, the door closed on a final scene of the sanctuary and the altar boy.

"We can skip the formalities. You're not here to confess," came an older man's voice from the other side of the partition. "You've not come in penitence, nor seeking salvation. Only relief. A release from what plagues you. After all, what absolution would you have received, had you taken your own life no more than half an hour ago? 'Damned if you do, damned if you don't' I suppose, yes?

"I'm Father Hearn," he continued. "You were sent to me because Father Talbot is no longer with us. 'Natural causes' and what not. Not *entirely* false. Though, perhaps *super*natural causes might be a more accurate assessment. Which brings me to why you're here. Why *you?* I'm sure you've been casting that question to the clouds for some time now. A question Father Talbot couldn't answer when he performed your 'exorcism' all those years ago. A question *I*, however, *can* answer for you.

"It's because you're no one," said the priest. "A nobody. No family, no friends. An insignificant, thirty-something, *Iowa* man that not a soul would miss if our trials were unsuccessful. Yes, to the world you are nothing, but to us you are of *paramount* significance. What surfaces in you is far greater than some mere demon. My colleagues and I have been planning this for some time now, and you are the *elect*. For, *through you*, my son, we will *turn the tide*. Through you, we will unleash *The Great Dragon*. Through you...we shall bring forth the Antichrist!"

A wave of shock washed over the man and his headache disappeared into the fray of fear and wonder. As he sat, paralyzed, he searched his clouded memories of the first possession: waking up on a gurney in a laboratory-like basement at St. Joseph's Catholic Church; the screaming headaches he's endured ever since; Father Talbot's strange disappearance. His mind raced as the priest continued.

"Yes, you are the vessel! A conduit for the Adversary! A prism for the true colors of our lord to be shown upon a scorched earth! A new dawn is upon us! Rejoice as the morning star ascends the horizon!" A clamorous thud resounded from the sanctuary like a battalion of soldiers snapping to attention, followed by a dark silence.

"Your head must be swimming," came the priest's recomposed voice, "'What will happen to me?' 'Am I going to die?' 'Will my soul burn in hell?' Perhaps somewhere in the recesses of your mind lie *theological* questions: 'Shouldn't the rapture happen first?' And furthermore, 'Doesn't the devil *lose*?' Well, let me shed some light on the subject. Flesh it out, if I may. We are circumventing Revelations through God's own fallacy. Did you truly believe Him to be omniscient? Why would He knowingly create an angel that would *defy* Him, tempt His beloved humans and then punish the humans for taking the bait? *Drown* them all for their wickedness, give them a second chance and still let them all burn for eternity? Minus the small fraction of His 'chosen' ones, of course. Does this sound like a loving god? No. It sounds like a god who is cruel, jealous, and most importantly... fallible.

"So, my son," the priest went on, "we've found a way to capitalize on His greatest mistake: giving mankind *free will*. After all, God's plan and man's volition could never coexist in the same realm. Instead of living for God, mankind has devoted its existence to industry and science, which have manifested the *perfect* avenues for our machinations. It's no coincidence that Lucifer was called the Prince of the Air, as it is through that very element that we shall materialize our lord in his earthly form.

"*Nonluminous matter* will be the portal. Dark energy the engine. They've been there from the beginning, yet we've only recently discovered their true purpose, and *you* contain our greatest invention. Five years ago a demon possessed your body and brought you to us. It recessed your consciousness while we surgically installed a chip into your cerebral cortex. The demon brought with it the unholy elements necessary to establish a pathway connecting the device's circuitry to the other side. A fractal bridge through the fabric of space. Hence, the headaches you've been enduring. It did, however, require a sacrifice. But mourn not, for Father Talbot is now a *king* in the underworld and will return as such at the right hand of our dark lord! As will you!"

Veins coursing with adrenaline, the man burst through the confessional door to find a completely different display than before. All of the pews were hovering all the way to the arched ceiling. The walls of the dark sanctuary were flickering with the flames of candles held by hooded figures. A pentagram of candlelight covered the entire surface of the floor. In the middle sat an altar and a table containing computers, cables, and what looked to him like some sort of laboratory equipment. The man noticed a red light beyond the far side of the stage that quickly came into focus:

EXIT

The man dashed across the sanctuary inhaling the aroma of melted wax, hearing nothing but his own heartbeat. Too afraid to see if the robed figures were closing in on him, he grabbed for the door handle and it gave with no resistance. The room backstage was as dark as his fever dreams. Slamming the door behind him, he dashed into the blackness of the room, when suddenly, the floor went missing from beneath his feet. Demonic faces flashed in his mind as he tumbled down the staircase before his momentum came to a crashing halt. The only thing he could see from the floor was a soft, glowing line of greenish white. The man caressed the wall for something to pull himself up with. Finally, his hand gripped a cold handle that gave way and the door swung open.

Fluorescent lights screamed into his eyes. All he could make out were two rows of black, monolithic shapes extending down the length of a long, bright room. Blue lights flickered on the monoliths and a dense hum filled the air. As he picked himself up from the ground, a tall, black-haired man in a dark suit and red tie appeared in front of him.

"Easy, son. Let's get you back upstairs, shall we?," he said with a cunning smile, and rested a heavy hand on the man's shoulder.

A cold shiver ran down the man's spine. He tried to lunge away from the black-haired man, but stumbled once more to the floor, sliding further into the bright room. The man in the dark suit looked down upon him and the computer mainframes on either side seemed to do the same. The man scrambled to his feet and decamped between the black columns. Another exit sign appeared on the far wall. He looked back to see if the suit was giving chase, but he hadn't moved. He merely stood there, staring, and his image seemed to glitch in and out like a hologram.

The door at the other end of the room had a long crossbar handle that clacked as the man forced through. A short set of stairs led up to another door that opened to the back lot of the church. Outside, a crisp, November wind swept his breath away and he halted, momentarily stunned by what stood before him. A maze of massive satellite dishes towered like gods reaching out to the gray sky. In one swift motion, the dishes simultaneously aimed their central arms down at the man's head. A chill cascaded down his back and he sprung forward. The satellites followed his every move as he weaved between the numerous mechanical giants. Soon, he arrived at a tall chained-link fence and scaled it like an escaping inmate. He jumped down the other side and rolled right into the oncoming traffic of 7th Avenue. Horns blared and tires screeched as cars hurled past him.

The man stumbled across to the sidewalk where bystanders stared at him with distorted faces. He ducked into an alley and spotted a young couple exiting through the rear entrance of a skyrise hotel. He caught the door just before it shut. Inside the hotel, white, vaporous fog was slowly rolling out of the base of each door extending the hallway. Desperate for a place to hide and catch his breath, he spotted a partially opened door halfway down the hall and scurried towards it.

Leaning his back against the wall, he peered into the room. It appeared empty but he entered cautiously. As he passed the bathroom to his right, the two queen beds came into full view. A large black dog was laying prostrate on the first bed with its head up like a sphinx. Startled, the man stumbled back into the desk. The animal didn't look at him. It seemed to not be looking at anything at all. As he stood frozen in place, the man noticed a blinking light coming from the other bed. He cautiously crept towards it, keeping his eyes on the dark beast. He took a quick glance toward the blinking light and saw that it was a cellphone. He patted around for the device while still clocking the motionless canine, and once he had it in hand, he brought it up into view. The screen was mirroring his own face in self-camera mode and three words were flashing off and on in red letters:

WE'VE GOT YOU

The hairs on his neck stood on end and his heart pounded inside his chest. He bolted past the dog and back into the hallway, at the end of which stood the man in the dark suit and red tie. At the opposite end stood a second man, identical to the first. He spotted an elevator lobby a few doors away and made a break for it. A group of people without faces exited the lift and the man slid past them. Once inside, he slapped at the panel of buttons and the doors slowly met in the middle, collapsing on a brief glimpse of a red tie and slick, black hair.

He was heaving for air and watching the red, digital numbers counting up floors when he noticed something twitching through his peripheral vision. He wondered what new horror awaited him. The elevator wall profiled a muted reflection of himself. His head was replaced with that of a long-horned goat, glitching in and out in ghostly strobes. He realised at that moment that his captors were moving forward with their infernal plans remotely, and he was almost out of time.

The elevator stopped at the 27th floor, the doors dinged and opened. A sharp ringing stabbed into his ears like kitchen knives and he stumbled drunkenly out of the lift. He dragged himself down the hallway searching for any form of escape he could find. An open door presented itself on his left and he was obliged to accept the offer. The room appeared to be breathing as the burgundy paint on the walls swirled in slow motion. His consciousness was collapsing like a dying star as he trudged towards the wall-length window. Outside, dark clouds were boiling above the tall buildings and he looked down to measure the distance to the street below. It would be enough.

The man picked up a desk chair and swung it at the window with everything he had left in him. On his fifth attempt, the glass finally shattered. Tears filling his eyes, he stepped onto the ledge. The storm clouds parted and in the blue sky hung a black sphere enshrouded by a blinding light that formed a ring around the center. The people on the street were going about their business, paying it no mind. Only he could see the singularity. He leaped.

As the street rose to meet him, the man looked upon the people going about their day: Two beautiful, young women waltzing down the sidewalk with shopping bags; a wedding party across the street; a tow truck driver lining up a haul. People of all kinds. People who never knew him nor ever would. They would never know his sacrifice. While his death may not deter this grand scheme forever, at least he could buy the world more time. Perhaps even provide a window for divine intervention. He could be useful for once in his life.

His descent was mere moments from impact, when the street dissipated in large, pixelated squares. The gray concrete and the city above it were replaced by black space filled with intense constellations of stars. The center of the galaxy was blazing before him and the sun, moon, and local planets were as clear as day. His body stood suspended in outer space with his arms stretched out on either side. Did it work? Had he sabotaged the schemes of evil men? Was he the savior? As he pondered these things, a great darkness consumed the light beneath him.

The man looked down to find the singularity was below him. Piercing light cascaded across the accretion disk and around the massive circumference of the sphere. The interior was blacker than a silhouette. Absolute nothingness. A complete quiet. His being stretched for miles as the event horizon pulled him in. The stars disappeared and all light vanished. Time stopped... and then there was fire.

The man's equilibrium returned in full as his body plummeted through the inferno. Waves of scorching flames snapped around him and the torrid heat burned like a furnace. Then, a figure began to form out of the flames that became a mirror image of himself in his nakedness. The eyes were the last part to materialize on the figure, and they met the man's gaze impassively. The figure's face contorted in agony as its head whipped back and it ascended, while the man fell farther into the pit of flames.

He watched the smoke rise from the exhaust pipe of a tow truck crossing under a downtown, Des Moines skywalk. Around him, people were walking, conversing, laughing. A wholesome, Midwestern wedding party cavorted by a sky rise wall that read: 666 Grand Ave. Two young women carrying shopping bags walked past him, flashing smiles in his direction. The man caught his reflection in the window of a hotel lobby and turned to face it. He ran a hand through his slick, black hair, adjusted his red necktie, gave himself a devilish smile, and strolled along into a ripe and unsuspecting world.

***

About the Author

A Cedar Falls native, Kevin enjoys high-fiving his dogs, talking trash to his son about sports, and room temperature Coke Zero. He's also a tattoo artist who doesn't like tattoo artists but loves tattooing and would love to tattoo you at Red Owl Tattoo 100 E. 2nd St. Suite 202 Cedar Falls, IA.

12

DEMONS FROM AHIGH

BY NICK NARIGON

The skull in the mud had horns. Little nubbins that poked out of its forehead

Oscar Mueller had never seen a human skull before. Chickens. Hogs. Cattle. Every animal you can think of. Oscar had skinned their hide and skewered meat clean to the bone. He'd scooped out brains. Now he was looking at a human skull. One with horns.

"Mother Mary," he murmured.

From behind him, Oscar's best friend Curdy stumbled out of the wall of prairie grass. Curdy let out a choked laugh.

"Fresh air!" he cried.

"Curdy," Oscar exclaimed. The cool air brushed over Oscar's ruddy cheeks. "Lookit this."

Curdy, a coquettish youth who looked as if he should still be reciting scripture in Sunday school, joined Oscar's side. Curdy let out a whistle.

He studied the skull, picked clean by carrion and bleached pearly white by the sun, sitting between them and the River Jordan.

"What do ya think it is?" asked Oscar.

"Well…" said Curdy. "It's a skull all right."

Oscar and Curdy stood on a rocky berm overlooking a gully. A wall of prairie grass as far as the eye could see lined both sides of the grassy gully. Down in the crevice Oscar could hear the trickle of water. Fresh water. Fresh fish were in there. Crawdads too.

"Who is it?" whispered Curdy, his gaze stuck on the horned skull. Curdy's hair had grown long like everyone else's, and he blew his sandy blonde bangs to thc side to get a better look at the skull.

"Think I know?" grumbled Oscar.

Heinie stumbled out of the prairie grass with the handcart rumbling behind him. He let the handles fall and the cart thumped in the mud. Heinie let out a bellow and stretched his arms toward the afternoon sun.

The rest of the crew caught up, bumbling Christoph bringing up the rear.

"Why'd we stop?" Christoph asked with a pout, leaning like a limp beanpole on Pastor John's shoulder.

"Lookit," said Oscar, pointing at the skull in the mud. It grinned as if the last words on its breath were a dirty limerick.

"Mother Mary," gasped Christoph, lurching forward from Pastor John's shoulder, tramping forward wildly, sprawling out on all fours to look the skull square in the eye.

"That's what I said," muttered Oscar.

"Who is it?" asked Christoph, whirling around to look each of his crew members in the bleary eye.

They stared back blankly.

"We don't know, Sir," stammered Pastor John. "He is with the Lord now."

"Or she," mumbled Curdy under his breath.

"Anyone see anyone?" asked Jacob. The bushy-faced handyman hitched his thumbs through the loops of his jangly leather vest festooned with iron knives, chisels, and awls.

"Nah," said Oscar, shrugging his shoulders, scanning the landscape.

The other side of the gully was nothing but the formidable wall of prairie grass.

"Some poor sap didn't make it past this," chuckled Jacob the Handyman.

"Too lazy," agreed the burly Heinie with a brusk har har.

"Is it... think it's a Shawnee?" asked Oscar, his gaze fixated back on the gaping skull.

'With horns?" asked Jacob, with another chuckle.

"Doesn't surprise me," clucked Pastor John. "The Shawnee are heathens. They have tails, too, pointy just like the children of Satan they are. Wouldn't surprise me if they had horns."

"Not Shawnee. Not this far west," said Curdy. "Probably Sac... one a Black Hawk's people."

"A heathen nonetheless," crowed Pastor John, quivering with fervor under his black coat and beaver-fur top hat. "We shall not dither over this obscenity of God any further."

"Absolutely right," squawked Christoph, who had lifted himself from his feet and was now striding toward the gully. The party followed him and looked down at the gurgling brook in temptation.

Christoph stopped at the reedy bank and jutted his scraggly finger in the air. "We mustn't stop. We move on. West. We must get there 'fore winter."

The team grumbled and shuffled down the bank of the gully. They ignored Christoph's protestations as they washed their faces and lapped up the cool water. It was Chrisoph who had gotten them this lost in the first place.

They filled up their canteens. They corralled sunfish and bluegills in a makeshift dam of rocks. Heinie gobbled down a wriggling minnow whole. Several minnows.

Finally, Christoph stamped his feet.

"As the leader of this expedition," he shrieked, his bony cheekbones splotchy red. "I insist we move forward at once."

The men, thoroughly drenched in the creek, filled to the gills with fish and water, trudged up the western bank and followed Christoph to the edge of the prairie.

Oscar's boots sloshed with water. He would probably get green rot between his toes. He didn't care. His eyes were clear and his chest burst with energy for the first time in weeks. He was ready to thrash prairie grass. He was ready to thrash Indians. Whatever stood in the way between this gurgling creek and Oscar's new Ioway homeland was but the walls of Jericho ready to come tumbling down.

Oscar skipped a step and hefted his rucksack higher up his back. The leather straps clapped and the buckle jingled. Oscar ran his finger along the line of the jagged leather stitching. The seal ran crusty like the incisions his mother sewed when Oscar's bottom lip was torn from dimple to dimple by a rutting boar he had the misfortunate of meeting during a berry hunt. Long healed, the lip still hung like a hunk of bacon.

It made Oscar think of Sabina. She always kissed Oscar on the nose because his lip was as numb as an ice block. He felt the small lump tucked in his rolled-up sleeve. It was a marble button that fell off Sabina's calico dress. He found the button in a crack in the floor of Farmer Girsch's hay barn. He caressed the button and dove headlong into the prairie grass.

He was glad he also brought a thick pair of canvas gloves. All day long Oscar swatted aside the towering prairie grass that stood between his traveling companions and their Ioway destination on the other side of the grassy sea. If you brushed a blade of grass just wrong it slit open your palm like a wicked papercut.

Injuries were a regular occurrence on the murky trail, but Oscar was a tough guy. During Friday night tussles back home at Bechsel's Grove he didn't give mercy until his teeth were buried in the dirt. He had the cauliflower ears to prove it. Thanks to a life of sodding dirt and holstering calves, short and wiry Oscar Mueller was tough as an ox and faster'n a coyote.

Oscar was also a good Christian. He kept his mouth shut. He kept his head down. He didn't let pride swallow his fealty. So he thought.

When tied together, beliefs and actions make a weak knot. Just ask Joseph wallowing down in that well.

It was three weeks, or maybe three months, since Oscar left Harrison County, Ohio with his team of friends and neighbors to settle new farmland in the fertile land of Ioway.

Their trek started out bountiful, gay even. The rolling summer hills of the Tuscawaras River valley bled across into Illinois. The land offered a bounty of fresh water, timber, and plump game.

They reached the mighty Mississippi in late summer when the water was low. They took the Keokuk ferry, which was nothing but two birch canoes lashed together.

Then they came to the sea of prairie grass. They'd heard rumors of the grass as tall as the timber and thicker'n granny's nether whiskers, but nothing could prepare Oscar for what he encountered.

They had been lost for days. Oscar only knew today was Sunday because Pastor John delivered his sermon during their Sabbath breakfast of beans and hardtack. They quit boiling the beans. Oscar stuck a dusty legume inside his cheek and sucked out the innards throughout the morning.

With beans in his teeth Oscar led at the front of the troop. He slashed at the relentless legion of prairie grass with a rusty machete fashioned from a wagon spoke. Oscar's childhood friend, Curdy Hinkel, was lock-step with Oscar, thrashing away at the grass, mowing down a sparse thoroughfare for the rest of the crew.

Behind them was Heinrich Buss and the handcart. Heinie was a hulking figure with muscles that bulged through is cotton shirt. The only guy in Harrison County that intimidated Oscar was Heinie Buss.

Behind Heinie was their jack-of-all-trades Jacob the Handyman who had fortified the cart with an iron mule harness padded with burlap that fit over Heinie's shoulders. From the rear of the pack came the familiar stumble of their leader and financier Christoph Bauer.

The son of Harrison County's miller and largest landowner, Christoph was sent off in search of new land to farm. Oscar suspected that Christoph's father didn't expect him to return.

Christoph suffered another of his fainting spells and crashed into the back of Pastor John, whose sole purpose besides delivering prayers before meals was to keep dapper Christoph on his feet.

Once again Pastor John caught Christoph before he flopped into the mud.

"We gotta keep movin'," mumbled the woozy Christoph, his hay-like hair glued with sweat to his forehead. "We gotta get there 'fore winter."

"Yer da 'un slowin's us down," grumbled Jacob the Handyman. Jacob jostled Christoph to his feed and gave him a nudge to make sure his feet were steady before they continued trudging forward. Pastor John held Christoph by the buttons of his waistcoat and guided him along until Christoph could continue his clumsy gait on his own.

Oscar and Curdy kept slashing away at the prairie grass, moving forward one mucky step at a time. What happened behind their backs was none of their business.

Their boots squelched in the muck. Locusts scattered under each step. Fat horse flies buzzed at their ears. At night mosquitoes swarmed in from overhead like demon knights of Baphomet.

Then from amidst the prairie grass erupted a scream. A woman's screech. It bristled the tips of the prairie grass and grinded into Oscar's temples. Somebody was in awful trouble.

"Less go," growled Heinie. Like a flea-bitten ox, Heinie, the handcart bouncing behind him, charged into the swath of prairie grass and was swallowed up in its arms.

Oscar and Curdy shared a glance. They raced after Heinie, Jacob short at their heels. There was no sound but the swish-swish of the prairie grass as they barreled forward.

Another ear-piercing scream. Louder. Closer. It sent shivers through Oscar. Teeth clenched, he hustled forward, his hand gripped on the handle of his machete. Curdy huffed and puffed next to him. Ahead of them, Heinie finally pushed through into a clearing.

This clearing was small. Round. Perfectly circle. Embedded by prairie grass on all sides. A conical sod hut, covered in grass like an old maid's bonnet, stood at the center. A fire pit in front of the hut smoldered with embers and curls of smoke.

The tortured scream erupted from inside the sod house.

Heinie bulled forward. His shoulders smashed through the grass frame of the open doorway leaving a billow of dust in his wake.

Oscar and Curdy once again gave each other a glance and darted after.

They squeezed through the door together. Oscar was struck with the pungent odor of feces. His eyes burned from acrid fumes. He covered his face with his forearm and turned to retch. When he opened his mouth the putrid fumes invaded, and his stomach churned.

Oscar leaned against the wall of the sod house, his elbow digging into the earthen structure. He kept his face buried in his sleeve until the fairies in his stomach subsided.

He came to when someone grabbed his elbow. He opened his eyes expecting Curdy.

He looked into the withered face of an old man. The man pinched Oscar's elbow with bony fingers. His sunken eyes and gaping toothless mouth were no different from the skull by the gully except for the yellow skin sagging from the man's hallow cheeks.

Oscar jerked away. The man, tattered rags hanging from his skeletal body, stood motionless, his crooked hand reaching out for Oscar's arm.

"Mother Mary," gasped Oscar. He scanned the open room of the sod house. Slatted beds lashed together with twine lined the walls. Another fire pit sat in the center underneath a stream of sunlight that came in through a hole in the ceiling no wider than Oscar's fist.

Oscar raised his machete out before him.

He saw Curdy still hunched over in the short doorway, his mouth drooping open, his wide eyes staring across to the other side of the hut.

Oscar followed his gaze.

There on the other side, seated on the slatted bench, was a shadowy figure. Its stringy black hair reached the floor, shrouding its body. The figure reached up with bony fingers and drew aside the hair like curtains.

Oscar saw its eyeballs first. They were yellow balls drooping from the sockets. The face was a mask of red blisters with the fringes charred black. A streak of white jawbone shone through a gape in the cheek.

The figure opened its wretched mouth and howled. The shriek burst through the hut with more despair than the children of Job.

Oscar huddled against the sod wall, fingers in his ears. The cool dirt coddled his cheek.

There was another pinch on his arm. Oscar peeked open his eyes. The skeletal man was gnawing on Oscar's bicep. The man growled like a mangy mutt as he tore at Oscar's shirt with his teeth.

Sabina's button popped out from Oscar's sleeve and dropped to the dirt floor.

Oscar gripped the man at the temples. He dug his thumbs into the spongy scalp. Oscar shoved back the head. The man tore loose of Oscar's shirt. Oscar shoved him against the wall like a ragdoll. The piercing scream continued to fill the room.

The skeletal man, whose face was planted into the wall, was saying something. His cracked lips were spraying spittle through his black-encrusted teeth. His voice hissed.

Oscar leaned in to hear, keeping one hand firmly planted on the man's noggin. The man gave no effort to fight.

"The Lord has taken away... the Lord has taken away," the man hissed.

Oscar leaned in closer to hear. The man's bulbous eyes captured Oscar's in a maniacal stare.

"Naked came I. Naked I go," hissed the man. "But don't go. Don't be. Don't be with them. Don't be naked with them."

"Who?" asked Oscar.

"The strangers," hissed the man. "The black demons... who alighted from ahigh."

Oscar backed away, releasing the man's head but twisting his shirt in a tight grip.

The woman stopped screaming. Everyone turned to look at the grotesque figure at the other side of the hut. Oscar was sure it was a woman in a gray cotton dress.

"Curse God," she screamed. "And die!"

The woman lunged forward from her seat. Heinie loomed out from the shadows. He swung a hammer. It crunched on the woman's back.

Oscar let loose of the man. He dashed out of the hut, pushing Curdy out with him.

They stumbled out together and gathered themselves in the afternoon sun, panting. Pastor John and Christoph looked at them agape.

"What…" asked Christoph.

There were bashing noises inside the hut. Clay pots rattling. Clods of dirt falling.

Then Heinie emerged. His broad chest heaved. His hammer hanging at his side. Blood dripped from the handle. Splatters of blood dotted Heinie's cotton shirt. Chunks of flesh stuck to his sweaty hair. His eyes were black.

"Les go," Heinie mumbled.

Oscar nodded. He hefted his machete, and he sliced through the prairie grass like the right hand of Moses parting the seas. They headed west as fast as they could, all silent except for Pastor John lowly reciting the Lord's Prayer over and over.

That night they found another perfect circle mowed out in the prairie grass. They figured the grotesque couple must have kept livestock here.

The crew added extra precautions surrounding their encampment. They erected their lean-tos in a row. They stoked the campfire bigger than usual. They staked sticks into the ground and wrapped ripped clothing around the tips—lighting them on fire as torches.

Thankfully the night was clear, and the extra fire kept the mosquitoes and rodents at bay. Oscar cleaned a bluegill and poked it on a whittled stick, roasting it over the fire. The flaky meat soothed his soul.

After the food stuffs were packed away Pastor John gave an extra-long sermon.

"It's days like these my brethren," preached Pastor John. "That makes clutch the Bible to my heart so the Lord can embrace my soul. And it is at the heart of the Bible where we will find our salvation. It is the most basic teachings of Jesus in which we can seek solace and comfort. The Sermon on the Mount is of course what I refer to. You have all heard me teach from the Book of Matthew... all of my favorite verses... Blessed are the poor... Blessed are the meek... Blessed are those who hunger and thirst... and Blessed are the merciful... for they will be shown mercy."

Pastor John paused and lowered the beaver skin top hat from his head revealing his receded hairline. Oscar and Curdy watched the fire that was being tended by Jacob the Handyman. Heinie stood in the shadows at the edge of the grass, breathing heavily through his crooked nose. Christoph sat at Pastor John's feet, his bright eyes enraptured by the sermon.

"What you won't hear me preach," continued Pastor John. "Is Matthew Verse 11. Blessed are you when others insult you... when others persecute you... when others speak evil of you... which is what we had down there today in that sodden house of sin. Those sinners spoke evil of you. They spoke evil of God. Satan was alive in that hovel, and well, Satan was smote. Crushed by the hammer of God. For blessed are we. Blessed are the pure of heart. When our earthly penance is done, the Kingdom of Heaven will welcome us with the same open arms they gave the prophets.

For we are the children of God. And in God's kingdom we will reap our reward. In Jesus' name, Amen."

"Amen," they all mumbled.

"Wonderful, Pastor," gushed Christoph. "Just wonderful. I do believe we will all sleep with warm hearts and clear heads tonight."

Christoph stood and led Pastor John to their shared lean-to. The others could here Christoph's voice as he continued praising Pastor John from underneath the canvas tarp.

"Heinie," called out Jacob the Handyman. "We oughtta turn in, too."

Jacob stood, dropping his poking stick in the fire. Heinie grunted and followed Jacob to their tattered lean-to.

Oscar watched the lean-tos as they subsided. Snores emitted from the open ends. Oscar and Curdy had first watch. Jacob the Handyman and Heinie would take second watch. They all knew Christoph and Pastor John had no intention of taking their early morning turn.

Oscar looked at Curdy, who was pulling his hair back into a ponytail and binding it with a long blade of prairie grass. When he had it tightly wound Curdy plucked something out of his breast pocket. He held it up in the firelight. It was Sabina's button.

"You dropped something," said Curdy with a churlish grin.

"Mother Mary," gasped Oscar, grasping at his rolled sleeve, finding it empty. He felt bumps on his bicep where the old man left teeth marks. He took the button from Curdy and rubbed it clean with his thumb. "Mother Mary thank you."

"Think nothing of it," laughed Curdy. "You'd do the same."

"If I lost this..." said Oscar, trailing off. "I... I couldn't continue. I'd chicken out right here'n head home."

Curdy laughed it off and turned his gaze to the fire. His pale blue eyes reflected the blaze. Oscar folded his shirt sleeve tight and returned the button to its fold, patting its small bulge.

"Sabina's all's I think about," said Oscar. "God I miss her."

"You miss her bosom," chided Curdy.

Oscar set his jaw grim.

"Don't besmirch her name," growled Oscar.

Curdy guffawed, and said, "She's got a good man, Oscar Mueller. You'll return to her one day. An' you'll bring her an' yer youngins' through this same prairie. Only then this here prairie trail'll be paved in gold."

"You really think so?" asked Oscar, suddenly wide-eyed. "Can I really bring a family out here. Inta this? What was that today? Did we see Satan today? Sure feels like it. Is this Hell, Curdy? Can I bring a family into this Hell?"

Curdy sighed and looked at his friend. Even after crossing five hundred miles on foot Curdy kept his baby fat.

"We knew when we set out there'd be days like this," said Curdy. "We'd see things we never seen before. Do things we never done before. I reckon... no one could imagine what we seen... what we did today. But we did it, and now we move on. There's gonna be other nastiness. You know it. I know it. At least now we kinda know what to expect. We ain't prairie virgins no more."

"No we ain't," muttered Oscar. He picked up a stray tip of prairie grass and stuck it between his teeth. After a spell of fire gazing Curdy continued speaking.

"Sometimes... I regret to say...," said Curdy with measured words. "I sin as well. I am a sinner."

"What in God's name are you talking about?"

"I envy," said Curdy, looking at Oscar. "I envy you. I wish I have what you have. Days like today in 'ticular. Lord how I wish I had someone at home. I wish I had someone thinking about me the way you think about Sabina. It would... it would make all this worthwhile."

Curdy's eyes moistened. He tried to hide a sniffle behind his sleeve.

"That's not a sin," said Oscar with a chuckle, ignoring his friend's tear. "That's life."

Curdy and Oscar laughed together. Curdy ran his hands down his face and mud streaked his cheeks.

"When we get back home," continued Oscar. "I'll fix you up. Sabina's cousin, Elise, she likcs you 'nuff."

"I s'pose," said Curdy, nodding. Then he looked at Oscar, his eyes glistening. "At least I have you."

Curdy let out a bark and Oscar joined him in another good laugh.

"I gotta go squat," said Oscar. He left Curdy behind at the fire and found a bare patch in the prairie to drop his drawers.

Later that night after Jacob and Heinie relieved Oscar and Curdy of their watch duty, Oscar had a fitful sleep. It was still dark when Oscar was startled awake by his dream, whimpering on the hard ground under his lean-to, his muddy boots sticking out from the bottom of his soiled blanket, rocks and roots poking into his back, the whisking of the hellish prairie grass torturously sweeping the inside of his roiling head.

He could hear Heinie and Jacob talking outside by the fire. Then there was a third voice. A woman's voice.

Oscar sat up and leaned toward the opening of the lean-to. He listened hard to make sure he wasn't still dreaming.

"Follow me," said the third voice. "I will show you."

Oscar heard the swishing of prairie grass. He heard clanking and clunking. He heard footsteps. The prairie grass went still. It was silent.

"Jacob?" Oscar called out

Nothing but silence.

Oscar crawled out from his lean-to. The campfire's flames were but curling fingers. The torches had all gone out. Oscar scanned the dark clearing. It was empty. He went to Jacob and Heinie's lean-to. It was empty. He could hear Christoph and Pastor John snoring.

He went back to his lean-to. Oscar crouched low and grabbed Curdy's foot.

"Curdy," Oscar hissed. "Curdy!"

Curdy stirred and cursed.

"What izzit?" grumbled Curdy.

"Jacob en Heinie is gone."

"What?"

"Jacob en Heinie is gone," Oscar said louder. Curdy sat up straight.

They soon rustled up Christoph and Pastor John. They found the broken prairie grass where Jacob and Heinie must have headed off.

'We can't go after them," shouted Christoph. "Not in this dark. Not when we don't know what's out there."

"Well I'm goin' after em," Curdy shouted back. Their fierce faces were sharp silhouettes in the dark. "You can stay here if you wanna."

"I'm going with Curdy," said Oscar, his jaw taut.

They could hear Christoph's teeth grinding in the dark.

"Fine," he said. "If we don't find them by dawn we return."

"Fair nuff," said Curdy, and without as much as a shake he and Oscar brandished their machetes and started hacking at the prairie grass, following the broken stalks left in Jacob and Heinie's wake.

"Honestly," Pastor John whined to Christoph as they followed close behind. "The devil is at play tonight and we are walking right into his trap."

"Most likely," growled Curdy, slashing away with his knife. "But without Jacob and Heinie we're good as dead."

The dank emptiness of the camp they left behind kept the party moving forward. After a bit of silent slashing and hacking they came to another circle in the prairie. They gazed about in wonder before plowing forward again. The crushed trail they followed became wider and more refined. They came upon another perfect circle surrounded by prairie grass. This circle was bigger.

The trail continued at the other end of the circle. The prairie grass was matted down like a woven rug. Jacob and Heinie didn't make that trail.

There was another people down that trail.

"Black Hawk," mumbled Curdy.

"We... we need to turn around," blubbered Christoph, clutching at Pastor John. "This is... dangerous."

"We ain't turnin' back," growled Oscar, his eyes blazing. "We ain't leaving Jacob and Heinie."

Christoph stammered. He swayed in the center of the circle leaning in heavy to Pastor John, the moonlight illuminating his pale face.

"It is a time for courage," said Pastor John, solemnly. "The Lord will protect us for we are righteous."

Christoph nodded glumly. The party forged down the trail, Oscar and Curdy blazing away, Christoph and Pastor John bumbling after.

They came upon more circles carved out in the prairie. They didn't pause anymore.

Oscar saw a black wisp gliding out of the corner of his eye, like a paintbrush whisking over the prairie. As they pushed ahead the black wisps became more frequent as if they were guiding Oscar forward.

Oscar glanced at Curdy. Curdy looked back and nodded grimly.

They finally came to the biggest circle yet. Big enough to hold a circle of wagons. The search party halted. A white orb hovered in mid-air. Black flames flickered on its tenuous surface. Oscar looked up and the clearing was covered by a black wire mesh.

"Satan's trap," gasped Christoph.

Internally Oscar agreed. He also thought about stabbing the orb with his machete.

Before he could do so the orb rose into the air. It flattened and they were encompassed in light. Oscar shielded his eyes.

"Hey!" someone shouted. Oscar knew that voice. It was Jacob.

Oscar uncovered his eyes. Sure enough Jacob had entered the circle, and the hulking Heinie was blocking the next trail.

"Jacob?" asked Oscar.

"Follow us," shouted Jacob.

"We've... we've got to go," said Oscar. "Go back."

"Yes," cried Christoph from behind, shrilly. "We must go. Now. I demand it."

The circle was bathed in light. The brightness drove Oscar to his knee. He squeezed his eyes shut. There were shrieks all around him.

There was a rush of wind. Oscar was jerked up by a force. His arms dropped to his sides. He dropped the machete, and his feet left the ground.

Then Oscar landed on his shoulder with a thud. It was dark again. Sprawled out, he felt the cool, matted prairie grass. He lifted his head and saw burning flames. Torches. Campfires. There were dark figures milling about.

Oscar searched for the machete hoping it somehow made this strange journey with him. It had not.

"Oscar," a voice hissed. It was Curdy.

"Curdy," said Oscar. "What in the Lord's name is going on?"

"We're not alone," said Curdy.

Curdy gripped Oscar by the shoulder and helped him rise to his feet. Christoph and Pastor John were also woozily gaining their feet and wiping dirt and grass from their coat sleeves.

Then Oscar saw that they were in a large encampment. There were grass huts and wigwams. Wooden stools and animal pelts hanging from racks.

They were surrounded by a crowd of roving figures. Oscar thought he spotted Jacob and Heinie moving among them.

"Shawnee?" asked Oscar.

"No...," replied Curdy. "I don't..."

Then the crowd erupted in cheers. Joyous cheers of whoops and hollers. Once his shock subsided, Oscar got a better look at the people surrounding him. He had seen Indians back home in Harrison County but always from a distance. The Lenape in Ohio had the recognizable deep-set eyes and beaked nose.

These Indians were as tall and lanky as Christoph with wide almond eyes and long slender limbs. As the crowd parted and the figures swarmed about Oscar saw that a towering bonfire blazed at the center of the encampment.

The Indians grasped each of their guests by the hand and led them to a giant dining table near the bonfire. Music of reed flutes and hand drums drifted in the night air. Dancers and musicians paraded around the fire in congruence with the enchanting tune. An olive-skinned girl with a white, beaming smile, led Oscar to a seat at the table.

"Hello," she cooed. Her silky black hair was braided with red and white beads.

"What? How do you know...."

Before Oscar could finish the word "English" the slender girl lithely danced away. Oscar spent more time perusing the crowed. The Indian men wore brown leathery loin cloths that shimmered blue in the firelight. The women wore bulky deerskin dresses. The hosts set dishes of putrid smelling food on the table.

"No thanks," said Oscar, shaking his head as a native motioned him to eat.

"Is this how they plan to kill us?" asked Curdy, pushing his plate aside.

"This is actually pretty good," said Jacob the Handyman who was scooping a pile of brown mush into his mouth. Oscar cautiously took a nibble. The mush was so sour that it was sweet. He ate until he could swallow no more. Then a woman poured drinks from a gourd chalice into goblets. Oscar sniffed the drink. Like the food, it smelled rancid. He took a sip anyway. It was a thin syrup that tingled on his lips.

The pretty girl who had spoken to him earlier gently gripped Oscar's arm and urged him to leave the table. They sat on the ground together next to the fire with the rest of the tribe. A weathered, gray man was wildly telling a story.

"Together Bon Ellowen Sic," he cried out, waving his hands about with a grimace. "Sic. Sic. We no sick no more. We make new. We make new blood. We sic... we stick... yes... we stick with the people. Stick with them. Stick. Stick. We no more sick. We stick together with new blood."

The crowd was enraptured in the wild man's tale. Oscar's head drooped and he blinked furiously. The sun should be up soon, he thought. He refocused his vision on the fire, but the people surrounding were a blur. The girl with the beaded hair was pressed against him tightly. He could feel every soft curve of her body clinging to him. He swiveled his head around and noticed that his entire troop had disappeared. Except Curdy. Curdy sat alone, entranced by the storyteller.

The girl led Oscar away once again. This time she led him inside a wigwam. Lights danced around him like fireflies.

"Hello," the girl said. Oscar was lying on wood-slatted bed. The girl stood over her him. Slowly, she lifted the lumpy dress over her head. Her body was slim and tight. An olive elf. Mesmerizing.

Oscar sat up as she seated herself on the bed next to him. Oscar's body went rigid. He thought of Sabina. He thought of their unborn child.

"I can't..." he stuttered.

The girl put a long, slender finger to his lips, hushing him. Her black eyes were engorged. She had a long jutting chin and thin lips puckered slightly. She clasped Oscar's hand in her other. She placed their hands together in Oscar's crotch. Her touch sent tingles through his groin.

Oscar's mind went blank. His cheeks went numb. His body moved of its own accord.

The girl leaned in and brushed her lips across the nape of Oscar's neck. The sensation sent swirls through Oscar's jugular. His lips parted and he let out a breathy moan.

He stroked the girl's hair as she continued kissing Oscar's neck. This was heaven. It must be. The girl clumsily fingered Oscar's shirt. He lifted her hands and unbuttoned it himself. He laid her down gently and laid on top cupping her breast.

She was a dark angel laying there in the shadows. Her long hair flowed behind her bare body like a cloak. She gazed at Oscar tempestuously, her unworldly large eyes fixated on his, welcoming him. Oscar unbuckled his belt and lowered his pants. His conscience was abandoned. He was but a carnal being bursting in the middle of a prairie on God's green Earth. The Lord protects and the Lord rewards.

Oscar leaned low over the girl and kissed her. He positioned himself and she spread open easily letting him inside.

Then a rough pair of hands jerked Oscar back by the shoulders. The girl shrieked. She curled to the side of the bed. Oscar swung his head around and he stumbled over his clothing.

It was Curdy. Curdy was dragging Oscar off the bed.

"They are all dead," shouted Curdy.

"What? Who?" Oscar blustered, pulling up his pants.

"Everyone! Everyone is dead!" cried Curdy. "We've got to get out of here!"

Oscar tugged on his shirt, leaving it unbuttoned. Thankfully he hadn't taken off his boots.

"Come on!" shouted Curdy. "We've got to go!"

Woozily, Oscar followed Curdy out into the stillness of the night. Complete silence hovered around the dying bonfire. Naked bodies were strewn about in the dirt. Not one Indian was in sight.

Oscar barely recognized the bloated face of Jacob the Handyman. Lying in the ash, his naked body was lumpy with blisters. There they all were lying in dirt. Their bodies covered in red boils. Yellow pus oozing from the open sores.

Heinie's giant body was like a bloated mattress. Christoph. Pastor John. Some deadly ailment had stricken them with a sudden brutality. Was it the food? If so, why were he and Curdy still alive?

"Come on, Oz," Curdy was urging. "We've got to run."

Oscar tramped after Curdy down the path through the prairie grass. His stomach was queasy. It gurgled. A rush of vertigo hit him and Oscar collapsed on the path. His legs were as heavy as lead.

"I can't," he said. "I can't go. I can't go."

"You can make it. We've just got to make it back to the stream," said Curdy. "You need water."

"I can't. I can't."

It felt like a mouse was scratching inside Oscar's lungs. His head swam. His face burned in waves.

"Come on," Curdy grunted as he heaved Oscar onto his shoulders. Curdy took a few unsteady steps then picked up momentum. He stumbled blindly for hours maybe until he crashed into the circular clearing where their lean-tos still stood. Curdy dragged Oscar into their lean-to and covered him with a blanket.

"Here. Drink this." Curdy dripped some water out of a canteen into Oscar's parched, white lips.

"Just hold on," murmured Curdy. "I'll get more water. You'll be safe here. Nobody's coming for us."

"Not... not...," Oscar mumbled as he tried to form words.

"I listened to the story," said Curdy, hurriedly. "They aren't Sac Indians. I don't think their Indians at all. They are, what did the old man say... strangers. Strangers. Black demons from ahigh."

"De... demon..." murmured Oscar. Sweat dripped over his cracked lips.

"The storyteller," said Curdy, rushing. "He said they came to mate. To make new animals."

"He...," croaked Oscar.

"Shhh," shushed Curdy. "Be still. I'll be right back."

Oscar dropped into unconsciousness.

When he woke again, Curdy was mopping his forehead with a wet rag. Oscar felt warm and flushed, but his wits had returned.

"Where are the others?" he asked.

"Everyone's dead," said Curdy, calmly.

"Dead? How?"

"Poison," said Curdy. "They were poisoned by the evil juices of the women. The demon women."

"The savages," cursed Oscar. Then he remembered.

"Sabina," he groaned.

"Don't worry," said Curdy. "You didn't get far enough. You didn't... finish."

"Oh...," said Oscar, his mind swirling. "Okay.... But... but what about you?"

"Everything's fine," said Curdy, setting the wet rag aside. "I'm okay."

"How come?" asked Oscar. "Why only you? You didn't bed one of them women? You didn't... finish... either?"

Curdy unknotted his ponytail. His blond curly locks bounced on his shoulders. He looked at Oscar with a sly smile.

"Well...," said Curdy. "I only love you."

"Oh," sighed Oscar, dropping his head to the ground. "Thank God for that."

***

About the Author

Originally from Cedar Falls, Hayseed Press co-founder Nick Narigon is a graduate of the University of Iowa School of Journalism. After more than two decades working in journalism in America and Japan, most recently in 2020 as the editor of Tokyo Weekender magazine, Nick moved to Singapore with his family where he finally pursued his dream of writing a novel. He helped found Hayseed Press in 2024 to help Iowa's talented writers pursue their own dreams of being published. Today Nick lives in New York with his wife and two sons.

13

BATTLE FOR MARENGO

By Alexander C. Bailey

Casper swallowed the last of his supply of coffee as he spotted the lone zombie shambling up his gravel driveway. With a sigh, he set his coffee cup down and picked up the homemade spear sitting next to the front door of his farmhouse.

He gave a loud whistle as he started walking towards the undead.

Like the other zombies he encountered, it turned to head towards the source of the noise.

Casper looked over the zombie, thinking about who it could have been in its life before death. Despite the signs of decay, Casper could see it was male. Its tattered khaki shorts and dress shirt were covered in dried dirt and blood.

Like every other zombie that had come onto his property, Casper made up a backstory for it. With no television anymore, he needed to find his entertainment somewhere.

He named this one Daniel. Daniel had been on his way to a job interview when he got bitten by what he thought was a homeless man. Daniel tried to drive home, but the bite made him pass out in his car, causing the vehicle to crash. Daniel was knocked out in the accident. Before he could wake up, the infection took hold, turning him into the undead monster he was now. Daniel had been wandering the Earth in search of food. Many days and nights passed before he reached Casper's place in the Iowa countryside.

Part of Daniel's skull was exposed on his bald head. Casper knew the bone matter on the exposed section was softer than the skull still protected by the skin.

Casper's usual tactic was to shove the knife end of the spear into the zombie's eye until he reached the brain.

Feeling adventurous, he wanted to switch it up this morning. Holding the spear like a baseball bat, he swung for the zombie's legs.

The undead didn't react to the pain, nor did Casper expect it to, but the blow had the desired effect. The weakened femur cracked, causing the zombie to fall to the ground.

The living man took a couple of steps back, watching as the zombie tried to get back to its feet. When it did, it toppled right back to the ground. The zombie tried one more time before it gave up. Back on the ground, the zombie used its hands to crawl towards its prey.

As much as he wanted to continue finding new ways to attack these things, Casper knew he had other things to do for the day.

He stabbed the knife end of the spear into the exposed skull, making sure to put all his strength behind it.

The zombie died with one last moan.

Casper pulled a rag from his back pocket to wipe the blade clean as he headed back to his house.

When the world was normal, Casper considered himself an amateur prepper. Living on a gravel road outside the town limits of Marengo, there had been many times he had been trapped for a couple of days by impassable snow. When he first moved out to his grandparents' farmstead, he added a small structure to the side of the house with good ventilation to house a couple of generators. He made sure to store enough fuel to power his essentials. Over the years, he hoarded enough food and water to live off of for extended periods. He never thought he would need it, but he felt better having it on hand.

When he saw that the normal world he was living in was on its way out, he increased all of these things as much as possible. He made sure to grab toilet paper and other bathroom supplies most people probably wouldn't think they would need during the end of the world.

As for weapons, he had a small stash of old shotguns, a couple of hunting rifles, a compound bow, and a .22 caliber revolver he inherited from his grandpa. Casper's dad had taken him target shooting a few times when he was a teenager, but beyond that, he didn't really have an interest in guns.

That changed when he caught the first glimpse of a zombie on the news. He wasn't much of a fan of horror movies, but he had seen enough to know what one of the undead looked like. On his trips to Cedar Rapids, he bought as much ammo for his guns as he could without raising any questions.

He was able to do all of this in the first few months after the virus escaped the quarantined city, River City, Iowa.

Casper felt pretty good and secure that he could now ride out the end of the world.

That changed when the criminals moved into town.

They took out the police force first. By this point, the state troopers were too busy dealing with the spread of zombies to do anything about the human invaders. A small group of townsfolk tried to drive the bandits from Marengo.

Casper never got the full story, but it was easy to find out what happened to them. The next time Casper went into town, he saw some zombies that looked familiar. Poles had been erected along both sides of the road leading into town from the north. The undead townsfolk, with thick collars wrapped around their necks, were attached to the poles by chain.

Casper came back under the cover of darkness to quietly dispatch them. He wished he could have cut them free from their chains, but fearing the criminals would come back at any time, he left the bolt cutters at home.

There wasn't a face he didn't recognize from around town. There were some he had even known since he was a kid, as they had gone to school together either a few grades ahead or behind Casper. His breath hitched when he spotted a couple he had hung out with for many years when he was in high school. Memories of seeing their kids grow up flashed through his head as he dispatched the married couple.

He could only hope the kids were okay.

After taking down the first five with his knife, he had to switch to his homemade spear. The upclose approach was taking too long as he had to swat away their hands multiple times before he could drive his knife into their skull. It was also playing hell on his sanity to stab familiar people in the face. At least from the back, he could imagine they were strangers.

By the time he was done, there were thirty twice dead corpses on the ground.

The entire walk back to his house in the country, he worked on a plan to get rid of the bandits invading his town. Casper knew it would take some time to put everything in place. He pulled on the knowledge he had gained from the military media he had consumed before the undead rose.

The first thing he needed to do was reconnaissance. Casper needed to figure out just how many criminals there were, if anyone in town had joined forces with them, where they were located, and what weapons they had.

With a plentiful supply at the farmstead, Casper would only go into Marengo once a week to go to the local bar, Ambies, for a single drink and to hear any gossip or news the local barflies would tell him. He continued this even after the criminals moved in. It seemed whoever was in charge of the group decided it was better to have a place where the townspeople could congregate in the open rather than in secret.

It also helped that a couple of the criminals became permanent fixtures at Ambies.

"Why the hell are you guys here?" Robert, one of the bar's regulars, finally asked one night after he had more than a few drinks, "I mean, I'm sure you have enough booze and drugs in that fortress of yours."

At the time, Casper didn't know what fortress Robert meant. He found out later that the criminals had taken over the courthouse in town as their base of operation.

"You know we don't like you, so why don't you fuck off?" Robert groused.

One of the two bandits, a man who never seemed to be wearing a shirt, got to his feet. When he stepped towards Robert, Casper was able to see that most of his body was covered in burn scars. The only part of his body that didn't seem to have been burned was his face, which was almost movie star handsome.

"If you have a problem with us, you could have just said something," the burnt man said in a low voice.

"Vulcan," the second man said as he set his drink down. To Casper, it sounded like a warning.

The man named Vulcan just scoffed. "It's okay, Tanner," he said. "Me and my new friend are just going to step outside and have a talk. Aren't we?"

Vulcan placed a hand on Robert's shoulder. Even though Robert's back was to Casper, he saw the man wince from pain.

"That's okay," Robert stammered, "I was just letting off some steam. I didn't mean anything by it."

"Letting off some steam, huh?" Vulcan said. In the low light of the bar, his grin seemed to twinkle. Some would say with mischief. Casper thought it looked evil.

"Come on, we can let off some more steam outside. We don't want to ruin the night for anyone else in here."

Vulcan waved his free hand, indicating the small crowd in the bar. It was as if he was challenging anyone to stop what was about to happen. When no one moved, Vulcan led Robert out the front of the bar.

No one else said anything, nor would they meet each other's eyes. They continued to drink whatever was in front of them.

A few jumped when they heard Robert begin to scream some minutes later. Only a few heard the whooshing of flames igniting some kind of accelerant.

Laughter could be heard over the screams.

Casper felt his hand travel to the knife on his belt as he caught sight of flames out of the corner of his eye. He saw a few others, not as many as he thought, look to the front window of the bar. The flaming figure of Robert was dancing in a circle as the flames burned away his clothes and flesh.

At the sight, Casper got to his feet, tightly gripping the handle of the large knife. He was about to head to the door when a hand fell on his shoulder. The knife was halfway out of its sheath by the time he spun around to see who was touching him.

"I wouldn't do that if I were you," the man Vulcan called Tanner said. "It's best to just let Vulcan play with his food."

"We aren't fucking food," Casper growled. The knife was still halfway out of its sheath. "We're fucking people. I know you don't care, otherwise, you wouldn't have invaded our town."

Tanner had a small smile on his face.

"If you'd been through what I've been through, then you would understand why we've come here."

"Why don't you try to explain it to me?" Casper said.

Tanner looked around at the patrons in the bar before he replied.

"When you've been living in Hell, a place like this looks like heaven," The bandit answered, "Besides, our leader told me he was from this town. Said it was time for him to come back home."

"Who's your leader?" Casper couldn't help but ask. His anger was starting to be replaced with curiosity. Casper had never seen the leader of the group of criminals.

"His name is Cade," Tanner said.

The name meant nothing to Casper. While Marengo was a small town, he didn't know everyone. That was just a myth people from big cities liked to believe.

When Casper didn't react to the name, Tanner just shrugged and continued. He moved to the bar, grabbing the drink Robert had left behind. No one said anything to him as he drank it.

"We stayed in the woods for a little bit as the infections spread. I wanted to come right here, but Cade thought it would be best for some of humanity to die off a little."

Casper felt his anger return as Tanner chuckled.

"You know we are the reason the River City Virus escaped the city. We blew a big ass hole in the wall. While the military outside was busy fighting the undead, we just slipped on by without looking back."

The image of running the edge of his knife across Tanner's neck flashed in Casper's mind. He had never killed another living person, but he didn't think he'd have any trouble doing it to one of the men who killed the world. He could feel the blade sliding out of the leather sheath. See it glint even in the low light of the bar. The skin parting as he slid the blade across his throat, letting the blood free. He'd move on to Vulcan next. Take the man down with as many stabs as it would take and then some.

Before Casper could even tighten his grip on the knife, Vulcan stepped back into the bar. The scent of lighter fluid and burning flesh wafted in with him. Those who looked at his entrance could see a small can of accelerant in his hand.

"You done?" Tanner asked, taking another sip of his drink without looking at the other bandit.

"Fuck, I needed that," said Vulcan, letting out a long sigh, "It's been a minute since I set anyone on fire."

He let out a chuckle that made everyone, besides Tanner, shiver in their seats.

"Tanner, it seems you have an admirer," Vulcan said as he strode over to Casper.

"He was just interested in where we came from," Tanner said without looking up from his drink. "He was just heading back to his seat, weren't you, friend?"

Casper stared at Vulcan for a few seconds before replying. He never thought he could kill all the bandits that had taken over Marengo, but he was hoping to take out a couple of them. After the events of tonight, he decided he would be happy to kill just one.

"I was actually heading home," Casper finally said.

"Stare at me any longer, and I'll come with you. We could have a passionate night together," Vulcan grinned.

"Sorry you're not my type," Casper said. He started to walk past his target, but the man put a hand on his chest to stop him.

"You sure about that?" Vulcan asked with a husky whisper. Casper felt himself stir a little. Despite what Casper had said, Vulcan was his type. If the man hadn't invaded his town and set a person on fire, he would gladly take him up on his offer.

Instead, he just continued walking. He thought Vulcan was going to keep him in place, but as soon as Casper moved, he removed his hand.

"Maybe next time," Casper heard from behind him as he walked out into the cool night.

The scent of a charred body hit his nostrils before his foot hit the sidewalk outside the bar. He felt bile rise in the back of his throat as he saw what remained of Robert in the middle of the street.

Casper did his best to keep it down.

He made it to the park across the street before he couldn't hold it any longer.

***

There was a house in Marengo that Casper had always been fond of. It was a two-story, yellow brick house located on Main Street. There was a good-sized backyard surrounded by a tall, chain-link fence. Blackberries had grown wild on each side of the fence. As a kid Casper used to pick a handful of berries on his way to the town's community pool located next to the house. One time, a woman had been in the garden on the other side of the blackberries. He didn't know she was there until she had spoken.

"Make sure to save me a few. I'm making a pie later."

Casper let out a yelp as he jumped. A few of the berries fell from his hand.

"Sorry, I didn't mean to startle you," the woman said with a light chuckle. She introduced herself as Vivian. Casper obviously looked guilty, and Vivian calmed him down without directly telling him it was okay. Finally, Casper hungrily ate some of the berries.

"All the kids in town, and even some of the adults, enjoy them," Vivian chuckled, "As long as they leave me enough to make a couple of pies, I don't mind."

After some conversation, Vivian asked if Casper wanted to help her in the garden. He nodded and spent the rest of the afternoon pulling weeds and harvesting the various vegetables and fruit. She sent him home with a bag full of some of the things he helped harvest. From then on, whenever Casper went to the pool, he would see if Vivian was in the garden. If she was, he would help her instead of swimming.

When Casper started junior high, Vivian's husband passed away.

Whenever he could, Casper would visit Vivian to chat and help her around the house. When he graduated from high school, Vivian was in the crowd with the rest of his family. When she passed away, he was one of her pallbearers. As much as he wanted to buy her house when her son decided to sell it, he just didn't have the money.

He lost track of who owned it over the years. When he moved into his grandparents' home after their own passing, he kept an eye on Vivian's house. When the dead rose, he saw that the couple that owned the house were leaving town. By chance, he caught them as they were loading up their car. After a quick explanation of what the building meant to him, they gave him a set of keys with the agreement that he would give it back when the world returned to normal.

Casper agreed, but he didn't know if the world was ever going back to normal.

The memories of Vivian broke his heart a little when Casper first walked into the house once its present owners left. It got easier the more he visited.

Even before the bandits came to town, he stashed supplies at the yellow brick house in town. He wanted a place to go in case he couldn't make it back to his house in the country.

It was where he went after leaving the bar after meeting Vulcan and Tanner.

***

Casper poured himself another glass of whiskey as he sat in the recliner in front of the fireplace in the yellow brick house. He kept a low fire going in the fireplace more for light than heat. Somehow, the bandits had kept the power and water on in the city, but Casper didn't turn anything on. The bandits were known to storm into any house with lights on to terrorize the occupants and steal anything they could.

He knew getting drunk wasn't the best idea after the events of the last few hours, but he really didn't care. It had been a few years since he had gotten really shitfaced. He felt it was overdue considering the circumstances.

The bottle was half empty by the time Casper passed out.

He was woken up sometime later by someone banging on the door.

Casper's eyes slowly opened as the banging continued. If he had been more alert, he would have shot up from his chair to see who was at his door. In his current state, he was just glad that nothing was crawling back up his throat.

He wobbled as he got up from his chair. The ground seemed to move under his feet. When he got his balance under control, he stumbled towards the front door of the house.

"I'm coming! I'm coming!" Casper shouted. When he reached the door, he yanked it open, ready to yell at whoever had woken him up. He hesitated as the sunlight blinded him. He didn't realize he had slept until the early afternoon.

"Casper, thank God you're still in town," a familiar voice said. When he blinked the light out of his eyes, he saw it was his best friend from high school, Austin. The pair had reconnected when Casper moved back to town. He was one of the people that Casper had confided in when the bandits moved into town.

"Austin, I don't mean to be rude, but I'm hung the fuck over. What do you need?"

"Great time to get drunk," Austin scoffed.

"You haven't walked past Ambie's this morning, have you?" Casper asked with a slight growl in his voice.

"I mean, I saw a black spot on the ground, but what does that have to do with anything?"

"They must have moved the body already," Casper said more to himself than his friend. When he saw Austin staring at him, he explained what had happened the night before.

"Jesus fucking Christ," Austin said, running a hand through his hair, "I think I need a fucking drink now."

Casper nodded, understanding the feeling.

"If you didn't know about Robert, then why are you here?" Casper asked. He realized just how dry his mouth was. He gestured for Austin to follow him into the house.

"There is a massive horde of the undead heading towards town," said Austin. "They're coming from the west. You can see the dust cloud it's kicking up from the edge of town. It'll be here in a few hours."

"Did you come here to warn me or recruit me to help defend this place?" Casper asked. He grabbed a glass from a cabinet and filled it. He drank the whole thing without stopping, only to refill the glass. This time, he sipped it.

"A little bit of both," Austin said, not meeting his friend's eyes.

Even in his hungover state, Casper knew what Austin was getting at.

"Quit beating around the bush and ask me what you want to ask me," Casper sighed.

"Is there any chance a few of us could hold out at your place until the horde passes? Some of us think it would be the best way to get rid of the unsavory types in town."

Casper had to admit he didn't entirely hate the idea. He knew rumors were going around town about the amount of supplies he had at his grandparents' house. So far, no one had tried to steal anything from him. He was thankful that he hadn't heard any rumors about the cameras he had set up around the farm. Casper knew when the internet finally went out, he wouldn't be able to keep an eye on his place when he stayed in town.

"How many?" Casper asked, sipping his water.

"Zombies or people?" Austin asked. Then, realizing what Casper meant by the look he gave him, he answered, "At least fifty if not more."

"I can't house that many people," Casper said, trying not to let his anger show. "Best I could do would be around twenty, and even then that's pushing it. Why don't we round everyone up to defend the town? Hell, I bet we could even get those assholes to help us."

"Casper, do you know how many people are actually left in town?"

Casper just shrugged. He knew people had been leaving for the last couple of months, but he didn't have an exact number.

"If the last count is right, we only have a little over four hundred people left in town."

The number made Casper choke on his water. He knew before the dead rose, there were close to twenty-five hundred people living in his hometown.

"Fuck me," Casper gasped, setting his glass down.

"Yeah. There have to be at least a couple thousand zombies heading our way. I'm thinking that's a low estimate, too. There could be hundreds of thousands."

"Do you know if there are any of those jumping kinds?"

In the few news reports Casper had seen, he learned there were two types of zombies coming out of River City. The first type was the run of the mill living dead that he had regularly dispatched at the farmhouse. The other type was something new. The camera didn't get a good look at the creatures, but Casper saw enough for his blood to run cold. They moved faster than the standard zombies and were able to jump great distances. The thing that terrified Casper the most was the sharp teeth and the talons they had instead of hands.

"They were still too far away to tell for sure, but if we're going to try and defend the town, we should prepare for them as well," Austin answered.

"So, have you changed your mind about running away?" Casper asked.

He saw his friend think about it for a few minutes.

"If we die, can I come back and kick your ass?" Austin finally asked with a sigh.

"As long as you don't try to bite me," Casper chuckled, "Come on, I'll get you a drink before I head out."

"You're going to talk to them, aren't you?" Austin asked.

Casper just nodded.

***

"And why should we help you people protect this town?" the man known as Cade asked, "Why don't we just let the zombies kill all of you?"

Casper couldn't help but hate how similar he had thought.

"None of you wants us here anyway," Cade sneered. "Do you know how it feels to not be welcomed in your own hometown?"

"Maybe you would be more welcome if you weren't complete assholes." Casper didn't realize what he had said until the words were out of his mouth. He let out a sigh, expecting a bullet to find his head.

Instead, the courtroom he was standing in was filled with the laughter of a single man. It was followed by the laughter of the others.

Casper opened his eyes, taking a look around the room. He did a quick count, coming to a total of twenty-five. There were mostly men in the group, but he spotted some women as well. Casper had seen more people wandering around the halls of the courthouse when he was brought through the building to the courtroom. Casper could only guess that this was just a small number of bandits in the town.

"That's a good one," Cade finally said as the laughter died down, "I'm told you had a run in with a few of my friends the other night."

"You mean that monster that set someone on fire?" Casper asked, "Yeah, you could say that."

"Vulcan is a unique individual, that's for sure. Did you know he was the reason we got out of River City? If it wasn't for him, we'd still be living in that hellscape."

"He's the reason the world is ending?" Casper already felt anger towards the man. Now that turned into pure hatred.

"Well, you could say that, or you could say it was the fault of the military for failing to contain the undead and the virus that they carry," Cade smirked.

Casper felt frustrated that they were even having this conversation. Austin was currently gathering people to help defend the town, and he wanted to join them.

"Look, are you going to fucking help us or not?" Casper asked.

Cade let out a chuckle.

"I'm getting there, just be patient." Cade leaned back in what was once a judge's chair. "Vulcan's usefulness has run its course. Truthfully, he has become more of a problem. Case in point, I don't approve of his actions last night. Sure, we will take what we want, but we need the people. Sometime soon, people will be the most sought after commodity on this planet."

"Thanks to you and yours," Casper interrupted with a snort.

Cade gave him a hard look that Casper returned.

"Be that as it may, I'm ready to make you a deal. If you beat Vulcan in hand-to-hand combat, I'll agree to join forces with you and the people of this wonderful town."

"And if I lose?" Casper asked.

"Then the town is on its own. We'll secure our building and clean up the mess when the horde passes, but if what you're telling me is true, then there may not be many people left."

"Sounds like I don't have much of a choice," Casper said. He had only been in one fight before, and it was nothing like they showed in the movies. His fight started with a headbutt and ended with his bar manager breaking it up. Casper didn't remember much of what happened in between. He had no idea if he was going to win against a hardened criminal like Vulcan.

"Not if you want our help, no," Cade said with a chuckle. Others in the room joined in.

"Well, shit," Casper sighed, "Let's get this over with."

Cade looked Casper up and down a few times before he pulled a walkie talkie out from a cubby in the judge's podium.

"Tanner, go ahead and bring in Vulcan."

"Roger that," Tanner's voice came back over the radio.

A few minutes of anxious waiting later, the clanking of chains could be heard getting louder and louder. All eyes looked to the large doors as Vulcan sauntered into the room. His wrists and ankles were chained together. Tanner was behind him with a short-barreled shotgun aimed at the man's back.

"I see we get to have our dance after all," Vulcan said when he saw Casper in the middle of the room, "Too bad we're going to have an audience."

"Had you behaved yourself, things could have been different," Cade said from his position above them.

Vulcan just shrugged, making the chains rattle. Tanner circled the man until he was standing below Cade.

"Someone going to unlock me?" Vulcan asked, holding up his arms.

Tanner looked to Cade. When the man in charge nodded, Tanner pulled a key from his pocket and unlocked the ankle chains first, then the wrist chains. They dropped to the ground in a pile.

"Weapons?" Casper asked.

Cade nodded to another man who tossed two large machetes onto the ground between the two combatants. The only experience Casper had with these weapons was picking them up at the big box stores in Cedar Rapids.

"What? We don't get to play with fire?" Vulcan asked with a joyless chuckle. He picked up one of the blades while kicking the other one towards Casper.

"You've had enough fire in your life," Tanner said. The shotgun was held loosely in his hand, but everyone in the room could see his finger was still on the trigger.

Doing his best to keep one eye on Vulcan, Casper bent down to pick up the second weapon. He stood back up just in time to see Vulcan swinging his machete in a downward swipe aimed for his neck. Casper stumbled back, feeling the breeze as the blade passed inches from his face.

He felt the grip of the machete in his hand. Vulcan was already coming in for another attack. Casper blocked this swing with his own weapon. He felt the vibration all the way up his arm. Acting purely on instinct, Casper lashed out with a kick aimed at Vulcan's groin. Casper heard the air rush out of Vulcan as the blow landed. Pressing the attack, Casper swung his machete at Vulcan's weapon arm.

The strike landed

The skin on Vulcan's forearm parted like a hot knife through butter. The wound wasn't as deep as Casper would like, but he was going to do better with the next one.

Vulcan took a step back. He looked down at the wound before smiling.

"Not bad," he said, "Savour it as this is the only blow you'll land."

Before he was finished speaking, Vulcan rushed Casper with his weapon raised for another strike. Casper moved to block it, only realizing too late that it was a feint. He screamed as he felt Vulcan's blade slice down the left side of his face. Gripping his weapon tighter, Casper dropped his shoulder before ramming it into Vulcan's chest. Blindly, he swung his weapon repeatedly into Vulcan's side. He felt the blade impact his naked flesh, but Vulcan's burn scars acted like leather armor, minimizing the damage. The insane man laughed.

Casper stumbled back as he felt the handle of a machete crack on the back of his head.

Both men stood apart from each other, catching their breath. Casper held his head.

"You're doing better than I thought," Vulcan said with a grin. He pressed a hand against the bloody wounds on his side and showed his wet fingers to Casper.

Casper let out a roar, channeling all the anger and fear inside of his body. He charged.

Vulcan responded by laughing.

The two men traded blow after blow. Vulcan had the strength, but Casper had the stamina. Vulcan's swings became listless. With one lucky slice across Vulcan's neck, it was over.

Vulcan fell to his knees as blood sprayed from the fatal wound.

The smile was gone from his face.

Casper stood over the unmoving corpse of his opponent, feeling no pain despite the numerous wounds he received. His shoulders heaved with heavy breaths. He knew he was never going to see out of his left eye again. He also knew that as soon as the adrenaline left his system, he was going to be in a world of pain. Some of the deeper cuts already started to sting.

None of that mattered right now.

He had won.

Dropping his bloodied machete, he looked to Cade.

"Alright then," Cade said with a large grin on his face. "Looks like we have a town to save."

***

Casper passed out after Cade agreed to help the town.

There were flashes of events that happened during his instances lucidity.

A couple of people patching him up and shoving pills into his mouth, forcing him to swallow them.

Being carried to a truck behind the courthouse.

The rumbling of the truck under his back as they drove to what he hoped was the defensive line of the town.

The truck stopped, followed closely by the sound of guns cocking and voices yelling.

"What the fuck are you doing here?!" Casper heard the familiar voice of Austin yell.

He heard Cade answer, but wasn't able to make out the words as the darkness took him again.

Casper shot awake when he heard a single gunshot.

Forgetting what had happened, his body reacted before his mind could. He felt his back hit something metal as he fell back. Feeling the bed of the truck reminded him of what had happened back at the courthouse. Casper looked down. He was wearing his bloody, tattered pants, but his shirt had been removed. His half-naked body and its numerous wounds were wrapped in bandages and medical tape.

He blinked a few times, wondering why his left eye wasn't working. Gently feeling his face, he found more gauze covering his eye. He pressed as hard as he could until the pain made him wince.

"Glad to see you're still among the living," Austin's voice said to his right.

"It doesn't fucking feel like it," Casper grimaced as every part of his body screamed out in agony.

"Well, as much as I liked to leave you here, we need every able body we got."

Casper nodded.

Austin helped Casper out of the back of the truck. Even the small drop down from the truck bed made the wounded man wince in pain.

There was a line of vehicles parked bumper to bumper on the highway on the edge of town. Four semi trailers were turned onto their sides with people standing on top of them. In front of the line of cars, two large excavators were hard at work digging a trench. They looked to have started at opposite ends and were meeting in the middle.

Casper could only hope that the trench was deep enough to help slow down the zombies.

There was a thick cloud of dust slowly getting closer and closer to the town.

"Come on, our command post is over here," Austin said as he helped Casper over to a parked RV. Two people were lying on their stomachs on the roof of the vehicle. One had a military sniper rifle to his shoulder. The other was looking through a spotting scope.

"Where did we get that?" Casper asked.

"Courtesy of your new friends," Austin snorted.

"Fuck you," Casper countered. The two men stepped into the RV. Casper could feel the tension thick in the air as he walked in. Cade and Tanner stood on one side of the RV. Ambie, the owner of Ambie's, and one of the town's remaining firefighters, Frank, stood on the other.

"You four getting along?" Casper asked.

The bandits chuckled while Ambie let out a grunt.

"Good to see you on your feet, son," Frank said.

"Thanks," Casper nodded. He opened his mouth to continue speaking, but the rumble of two loud engines cut him off.

"Guess the boys are done waiting," Tanner said. He moved towards one of the windows facing the oncoming horde. He pulled the blind open so all six people could see the source of the engines.

Two muscle cars covered in metal plating and barbed wire drove towards the horde of undead. They were side by side for most of the drive, but for no reason other than to show off, the two crossed each other. The pair broke off, one going left and the other going right. Gunfire could soon be heard echoing towards the defenders.

"Those boys are going to thin out the herd a little bit," Cade said. Casper saw he had a large grin on his face.

Wanting to get a better view of the destruction, Casper headed back outside. Austin, Ambie, and Frank followed him.

"Are you sure we can trust these guys?" Ambie asked when the small group was a few cars away from the RV. Explosions made them all jump.

Casper caught sight of a small green object flying out of the driver's side window.

"Fuck no," Casper replied. "But I have a feeling without them we don't stand a chance."

"The enemy of my enemy," Frank added.

Casper nodded.

"Cade explained what you did for us," Ambie said, "I don't know how we, or this town, can ever thank you."

Casper just waved her off. There was no way he could properly explain that this was his home. That he would make a deal with the devil himself to save it.

He felt like he already did.

With help, Casper climbed onto one of the semi trailers. Austin backed his truck up as close as he could to the trailer as possible. The plan was that if the line was going to be overrun that Casper would jump into the bed, and Austin would drive him up and down the line covering the retreat of others. Frank and Ambie joined them on the trailer.

The muscle cars drove back and forth in front of the oncoming swarm for another half an hour before the cars had to retreat. A great number of the mutated jumping zombies converged upon both vehicles. Not wanting to risk hitting the drivers, none of the human defenders shot at the cars. The car on the left was able to shake the zombies free. The other tried, but swerved too hard, causing the vehicle to roll three times before coming to a rest on its roof.

The screams of the dying men could be heard over the moans of the dead.

Thankfully, they didn't last that long.

While all of this was going on, the excavators were still hard at work digging the trench. The machines grew silent as they reached their end points. The trench wasn't as deep as Casper would have liked, but it would suffice.

The trench could slow the normal zombies down, but wouldn't completely stop them. When there was enough to zombies to fill the trench, the rest would just crawl over them. The trench couldn't do anything to slow down those jumpers. Casper only hoped that the rest of the defenders would target them first.

According to Austin, there were around two hundred people spread out along the highway. Most of the rest of the townsfolk were held up in the high school with all the kids. Some decided to try their luck in their own homes.

The first line of the undead horde was half-a-mile away, trudging through the harvested cornfields, when the sniper on the roof of the RV started firing. Casper heard two other rifles shooting as well. He wondered just how much military hardware Cade and his people had. It was something he would have to find out if they survived the next few hours.

Casper watched as the sniper picked off a number of the jumpers. This was his first experience with these horrific things. It was encouraging to see they could be taken down with body shots as opposed to the requisite headshots like the garden-variety zombie.

When the horde of zombies was a few hundred yards away, automatic weapons started firing.

Austin handed Casper a familiar hunting rifle with a scope on it. When he gave Austin a look, his friend just shrugged. There were also two familiar green ammo tins on the trailer.

"Here we go," Casper said as he lay on his stomach next to his tins before putting the stock of his grandfather's rifle to his shoulder. Knowing he could never hit a fast-moving target, Casper aimed the crosshairs of the scope at the middle of a shambling zombie's head.

Firing his first shot, Casper joined the battle for his hometown.

The zombie's head snapped back as he hit his target.

Before it hit the ground, Casper shifted his aim to another undead.

More hunting rifles were fired as the swarm was now in range. Those with pistols and shotguns would wait until the undead reached the trench before shooting.

Unlike the other times he had killed zombies, Casper felt a sort of detachment from his emotions. These zombies had no names. His shooting became almost robotic.

Aim

Fire

Aim

Fire

Aim

Fire

Aim

Fire

Aim

Fire

Reload.

Aim

Fire.

He pulled the trigger so many times that his finger got sore. By the time he was out of ammo for his rifle, the pile of twice dead bodies in the trench was so tall that the still oncoming zombies could stumble right across.

Casper grabbed the sawed off, double-barrel shotgun he had kept above his front door. It wasn't the most practical weapon for this situation, but the rest of his guns were being used by others.

The air was filled with the mixture of gunfire, moans of the undead, and screams of the living. When those with no backup weapons ran out of bullets, they used their guns as clubs. Others used anything from baseball bats to golf clubs to fight back the undead that reached the line of cars.

The jumpers began to leap over the cars. Casper was pleased to see the ex-military townspeople were handling the jumpers with the automatics Casper had kept stored in his grandparents' basement.

Not a single defender was free of blood splatter by the time the battle was over.

"We did it," Austin gasped as he fell onto his ass with his back against the semi trailer.

"Yes, we did," said Casper, following suit.

They were surrounded by zombie bodies.

Casper once again felt his muscles and injuries grow sore.

"I'm going to sleep for a fucking week," Casper said.

"We'll have to clean up the bodies first," Austin said, "Frank and Ambie are getting a count of how many of us are still alive. Once they're done, we can start planning on what to do next."

Casper nodded. With everything, he was starting to feel like he was in charge of the remaining citizens of Marengo. It was something he never thought about before, nor did he really want the responsibility. It was something he would have to figure out later, as two people were walking towards him.

"We part of this town now?" Cade asked with a smirk on his face. Tanner stood a couple of steps behind him. Like the rest, they were covered in blood and gore.

"Not even fucking close," Casper said. Despite how exhausted he felt, his remaining eye burned with hatred.

Cade nodded, the smirk still on his face.

"Well, we will just have to do what we can to change your minds," Cade said, "But for now, I think a few days of peace is in order. We'll leave you alone to lick your wounds."

Cade grinned before heading back the way he came. Tanner gave them a nod before following.

Casper let out a long breath as he watched them go. He let his anger out along with the air from his body.

He knew he was going to have to do something about them soon.

Just not today.

Today, they needed to celebrate the victory.

Today, his hometown was safe.

***

About the Author

Alexander C. Bailey is a bisexual horror author from Iowa. He is the author of the Fall of River City series, as well as has multiple stories published in several anthologies. If you would like to get to know Alexander, follow him on Twitter @AlexFromIA or on Bluesky at alexfromia.bsky.social. He can also be found on Goodreads and Amazon under Alexander C. Bailey.

14
BROOD PARASITE

By Wes Smith

You wake up to a warm, welcoming sunrise. Your wife gets up before you, being as gentle as possible to avoid waking you. You look out the window, the fields beyond the horizon gently blowing in the morning wind. You get out of bed and quickly get dressed. You walk towards the bathroom to see your wife taking a bath. She likes to get clean and ready before heading out for the day. You don't linger, you're a gentleman after all. You finish your morning routine. You walk downstairs to see your son, feeding the pets. His dirty overalls suggest that his morning chores are already done. You've always been proud of him; he's hard-working, respectable, and he learns from his mistakes. Something he didn't get from you, so you follow in his example. Your son sees you and runs up to you. His small body clings to your leg. He has your silhouette. You pick him up and hold him close. You play with him for a little bit, and your wife walks downstairs. Her dress and matching bonnet are only a fraction of how truly beautiful she is. You step away from your son to kiss her. Your son excitedly takes her hand. It's almost time for the festival. The festival when God comes down and takes the holy few. You were planning on going with them to town to pick up a few goodies, but you've made the last-minute decision to do some work on the farm. Your wife and son respect your choice, but your wife checks to make sure this is what you want. You tell her yes and that you'll see her later. That's the first and last lie you've ever told her. In all honesty, you're not sure, and you know you won't be seeing her again. But this is something you have to do. She kisses you, and they head out for town. After you watch them leave, you begin your work. You take the pet's bowl that your son filled and dump it out. You look out near the end of the field and imagine what corn looks like.

Instead, all you see are weeds and invasive plants. The will of God crawls down your spine, and you know it's time. You turn your head to see a man. You can tell he looks like how you're supposed to look. His head is bleeding, messy hair, dirty clothes, his pants are torn, and his eyes. Their eyes or what you'd imagine your eyes to look like. You look down at his hands. His right hand grips a brick. Probably found it out back next to the fallen barn. He's gripping it so tight his fingernails are dug into and they're bleeding. You look back at him, his face gives away to a feeling you've never seen or experienced but have been taught. Taught to you by God. A feeling he has told you that you'd feel once you've hatched. You put your hands up and slowly, gently, calmly, walk towards him. He has your silhouette. CRACK!

***

The cold fall wind gently waves and floods the small Iowan town. The air swirls into the windows of the small apartment where Cain Anderson sleeps. The thin blanket and uncomfortable couch do little to keep it from worming its way to his skin. Cain's goosebumps spread through his body like the thorns of a rose, causing Cain's discomfort to grow higher than it already was. His eyes slowly open to the morning sun rising over mockingly to his friend's AC-less apartment, taunting him with its warmth. Frosted air punishes Cain from the open window. Cain rolls off the couch and locates his phone on the other side of the room, where the only living room outlet is. He looks at his text messages. "Mary, please don't leave. Don't take my family from me, I beg you." The icon next to the text indicates "unseen." Cain wanders back towards the couch and sits down on it with a thud. Head in hands, the sound of his friend slowly waking up in the next room is the only thing joining the choir of his misery. The mocking morning sun opens up with what is clearly meant to be a beautiful day: the chill breeze gently blowing the leaves off trees, the stirring of a friend nearby ready to take on the day, and the silence of a woman who's had enough of him.

David walks out of his bedroom to see Cain, head in his hands. David isn't fully sure what had happened, but Cain had been in a tight spot for a while. He and his wife had recently divorced, and just a couple of days ago she won custody of their child. David didn't know the full details; he tries to ask now and then, but it always causes Cain to drink. David didn't want to think about how those things could be connected. David looks out at the main street. Both of them were raised in Grundy Center and grew up together. The small Iowan town, like most small towns, isn't a stranger to people down on their luck. From David's perspective, it has a weird effect of attracting people like that to it. Maybe not on the surface, but David knows better. Most of his family and friends hit rock bottom and then somehow end up here. But unlike Cain, most pick themselves up afterwards. The town is also weird in that way, where it always helps someone pick themselves up, even at their lowest.

How or why that is the case, David isn't sure; maybe it had something to do with people wanting to leave? Or maybe something to do with its atmosphere. Either way, it isn't helping Cain.

David looks at the clock on his wall and sees that it's near time for him to leave for work. He works all the way in Waterloo, which meant leaving Cain alone in the apartment for a decent amount of time with no real way of getting back quickly if something happened, which normally isn't an issue if not for the state Cain's in.

Looking towards Cain fills David with a sense of worry that he'd only experienced one other time in his life. One of Grundy Center's locals, a man named Abraham, disappeared more than ten years ago. A feeling crawls up and down David's back, a similar feeling he gets when he prays at church. David takes it as a good sign, but his faith wavers.

"Hey, Cain, buddy, I'm gonna head to work. Are you gonna be okay?" Cain didn't make any reaction or movement in David's direction but gave a subtle nod. David didn't believe or trust him, but he'd already taken more than a few days off to help his friend. If David didn't get to work, then he wouldn't have the money to pay for the apartment they were both now using.

What concerns David the most is that Cain's wife is most likely leaving today to head out of state for good with their kid. David had to convince Cain not to go running to them and get himself in trouble. But now he could only imagine how much worse that urge must be.

"Alright, buddy, I'm gonna head out. You stay here or maybe go for a walk. Go on a trip down memory lane. You remember that one house that puts a skeleton in the attic every Halloween. Well, it might be up early this year. Go take a look at it, you know, like we used to."

Cain just sits there ignoring David's words.

"Alright, if you need anything, call me."

David leaves. The sound of the closing door takes Cain back to Mary: her words, her anger, and her face. Cain's regret boils inside of him like magma melting away at his flesh. No tears come out as they turn to steam in his veins, fueling another level of wrath he'd try to hide. It was one mistake, and she had to take their child away from him. That's extreme; no one deserves that. How could Mary do this not only to him but to their child? They need a father in their life! Not only that, but Mary loved him once, didn't she? And now one small mistake causes her to change up so suddenly! Cain's thoughts grow angrier and angrier. His failure to calm himself down begins to make his mind roam even more, causing wrath, which stems from regret. Then turns into blind hatred.

Another gentle breeze blows through the window. Cain directs his eyes towards the window; the sunny, beautiful fall day shines happily. Kids with backpacks walk to their schools deeper into town, some on bikes, some with friends, others with siblings. This makes Cain think of his kid and how his now ex-wife is pulling their child away from their friends and everything they've known. All because of one mistake!

The day outside continues to mock Cain with its beauty. Cain sits there, scanning across the coffee table in front of him, something that had become a nightstand for him in the past weeks. His keys sit there on the edge like the sword in the stone. They are his holy weapons, which he can use to reclaim his family and his kingdom.

It doesn't take long for Cain to decide where he is going. He knows where they are and where they are going. At least he has a pretty good guess. Mary doesn't have much family, so there is a good chance that she'd go somewhere close to them. Cain drives and drives, driving through small town to small town. The welcoming sun and fall air that he drives through does nothing but add to his rage. Cain knows that after everything, he is being mocked, made fun of, even by the world around him. But he is going show them, he is going show them all. He has to. This is his last chance to become the person he always wanted to be. A good man, a good husband, a good father, and someone worth being cared for.

The corn field stretches from horizon to horizon as he drives. Like a sea of endless vegetation and familiarity. He'd grown up around these fields; he knows them and they know him. The fields sway in the breeze, making them appear as a cheering audience, making Cain feel a strong sense of comfort. Cain fails to realize that they aren't cheering for his success.

Cain doesn't notice the drive is taking longer than usual. The serene scenery rolling by does nothing to calm the burning in his blood. The rubber keeping him from high-speed asphalt is quickly eroding. Something is eating away at the rubber to a dangerous degree. As Cain's impatience grows, he slams on the gas one last time. POP!

A deep, jagged, pained breath enters Cain's lungs as the ringing in his body tries to catch up with the pain in his skull. The first sight Cain sees in the dawn of the rising sun is smoke pouring from under his car's hood. Then he sees the car is halfway fused with a tree. The tree stands tall and strong, judging Cain for the accident. Cain examines himself and finds no injuries except for some bruises here and there. Forcing himself out of the remains of the car, Cain scans for his phone. The beginning of a new day rises. Cain questions how long he'd been out there. He'd left early in the morning, but now it appeared to be a new day. Could he have been out all day and night without anyone finding him? The oak trees swirl and laugh in the wind to Cain's thoughts. Leaves fly down to the welcoming ground like a falling bird. Empty nests with empty broken bird shells rest inside like a graveyard of innocence. The vegetation that Cain has only experienced a few times in his life surrounds him like a predator waiting for him to walk. Like a flytrap, something calls out to Cain. The pine needles fall to the ground in the wind for the small chance to pierce Cain's feet as he walks. Despite a wary sensation, Cain walks to the edge of the woods.

****

In Cain's mind, the pain becomes an afterthought just as the phone did. The reality of his location and its impossibility draw his attention away. Something about the area calls to him, even if he didn't notice it. He looks back at his car, and for a split second, he thinks about leaving it behind and going deeper. Into where and what didn't bother him nearly as much as it should have. But his mind goes back to his son. Cain looks for his phone in the tall grass. More time passes as the sun rises higher in the sky. Mother Nature is fully awake. He finds his phone smashed to pieces from the accident. It did nothing to calm Cain's thoughts. A sick feeling overcomes him, a feeling of worry, regret, anger, and dread that Cain only felt once in his life, and that was when Mary asked for a divorce.

Cain sits down on the ground, his eyes glued to the ground as his thoughts wander. His dread, regret, and worry begin to boil over again into rage. He can't fathom being punished again so severely for one mistake. Though this time around, there is only one person to blame in Cain's mind. God. It has to be his fault for everything bad happening to Cain. If he hadn't been punishing him so severely for minor mistakes rather than something reasonable, he wouldn't be here. He wouldn't have almost lost his life, he wouldn't be losing his son or wife, he wouldn't be here.

Getting up finally, as the sun slowly leaves the horizon behind, Cain fails to notice it is already mid-morning. He walks straight into the woods in hopes that it takes him to the road. Walking through the brush, the trees get thinner and a farmhouse slowly begins to shine through the trees. Cain pictures the possible interactions that could happen, with him coming out of the woods. Looking down at himself, his clothing is ripped and dirty. Not to mention the fact that he probably smells. Though the truth is the truth. Cain imagines that being honest is the best thing to do. Cain sees someone who he guesses is a child by their size. Their dirty overalls and boots match the fact that they're throwing what looks to be some type of feed around an empty animal pen. The pen being empty, though, isn't the first thing to catch Cain's attention. It's the child themself.

The child's fingerless hands reach into the bucket, and like a magnet, the feed sticks to them. As the child makes a throwing motion, the feed flies off. Their featureless head looks around to make sure there isn't one piece of the pen that hasn't received the feed. The child's dirty clothes make it seem almost human, but it's only the shape of one. The smooth surface of their whole body isn't smooth like skin. It seems to be rough and hard. The creature's skin appears to be more of an egg-white shell than skin. They move with smooth motions and a childlike speed. Despite its body looking like that of a fragile mannequin, it moves like it's a real blood child. Cain creeps closer, unclear of why he was moving in despite his fear. Something makes him feel sick, a sickness that needs him to find something, but he can't figure out what. Cain scans for a possible weapon but finds nothing. Until he notices an old barn that has fallen on the edge of the property. Cain notices that a pile of loose bricks is mixed with the rubble. Cain picks up one of the bricks in his right hand for protection. He glances back at the house, and the child-like thing now in the house is visible through a window. Another one, a bigger one, walks down the stairs. It looks just like the child, except its shell-like skin is even whiter. The big one picks up the small one and spins it around.

Cain is taken back to his child. Visions of him playing and caring for his child flash through his mind. Cain sits there and watches the creatures play games and have fun. He can tell that they're enjoying themselves despite their lack of eyes and mouths. Tears begin to pour out of Cain's eyes as he tries to stay quiet. Then another one of them comes down. This one looks just like the others, except its shell skin is a darker color, and it's wearing a beautiful yellow dress with a bonnet on top of its head. The creature that Cain assumes to be the father steps away from his child to receive what can only be assumed to be a kiss from the one in the dress.

In the moment, something boils up inside of Cain. His tears fade away into a happiness, a joy he hadn't felt in the past few months. A joy he felt when his child had just been born and everything was perfect. Cain watches as the three creatures have some sort of conversation that he can't understand because no sound comes out, but he can somehow read their body movements. The joy of watching this family begins to sour as the father gently places his hand on the mother's face. Cain can't read what is being said but is shocked to watch the mother gently float towards the exit of the home while the child excitedly follows. The father just let them leave. Not only that, but he looks proud because of it. Are they coming back? Is he just letting them go? How does he know they'll come back? Does he not realize that if he doesn't go with them, he'll surely lose them! Is he mocking me? Does he think that I'm not strong enough to get my family to come back, and he is? What makes him think he deserves a perfect family more than me? I'm strong, I'm the strongest, I just made a few mistakes people keep overreacting about! And here this bastard is mocking me! He still has his family, and he's even letting them go by themselves! That's what it has to be! Cain's thoughts cause his blood to roil inside him. His vision goes white with wrath as the father goes about doing various things in the yard. Cain finds it pathetic because the father isn't even doing anything, just standing around and throwing things away. The brick in Cain's hand feels hot as his nails dig into it. Blood boils out of his fingers and nails as he grips the brick too hard in anger.

The father walks outside and proudly looks over a grown field of nothing in particular. Cain walks towards him, stopping to see if he notices. It doesn't take long; the father turns around and looks Cain in his eyes with his featureless face. The father calmly put his hands up and walks towards Cain. His calm behavior sends Cain over the deep end. Running at full speed, Cain slams the brick into the father's head with all his strength. The father's head caves in and explodes into shards almost instantly. Some thin film helps the pieces stick together but doesn't prevent them from being cracked open. A clear, thick liquid comes out of the creature's head. The smell is almost metallic but not strong. Almost like blood watered down a hundred times. The father falls instantly, collapsing towards the ground with a hollow wet thunk.

"How's that?! Does it feel fucking good!? Don't ever assume you're better than me! I'm better than you! I always will be!" Cain yells at the lifeless, leaking shell. Cain picks up the lifeless husk and finds an empty shed, and throws it in. He examines the entity and sees another thicker yellow blob slowly trying to pool out of the creature's body. Cain throws his brick at it, causing it to burst and deflate. His smile matches the sickness he felt before killing the creature, which had now been cured. Cain slams the shed door shut. He feels his excitement building. He walks towards the house, finding a pair of fresh clothes. He admires the home and its cleanliness. Cain buttons up the stolen shirt and walks downstairs.

He's greeted with a tight, small hug around his legs. The child and mother are back, and they carry baskets of what seems to be various meats. Cain picks the child up, and they cling to him with excitement. The mother comes up to him and places her lips, or most likely where they would be on her face, to his cheek. Cain looks at the child and smiles. He'll be better than that thing was. For the rest of the day, Cain plays with the child and helps the mother around the house, and none of them seems to notice he isn't their original family member.

Night slowly falls for them. Eventually, Cain puts the child to bed. When Cain climbs into bed with the mother, he doesn't stop to think how strange this is. How just yesterday he had his own family to get back, instead, he simply stole another. Lying there in bed, his mind can't focus on anything except a pain in his right hand. He lifts it up, and in the moonlight, sees the dried blood from the brick earlier. Cain smiles. The price for a new chance is simply a slightly hurt hand. He thanks God for finally giving him the rewards he deserves for everything he's gone through.

Cain's sleep is dreamless but happy. He wakes up excited to have another day with his new family. And that's how it goes for a while. Cain wakes up and spends time with them. He plays with his son, making sure to be careful not to crack him like he did the father. He romances and kisses the mother. Cain does everything he can for them. Now and then, when neither one is looking, he goes to the shed and gloats to the empty dead husk, whose insides are slowly coming out and turning green.

***

One day Cain wakes up and finds the mother taking a bath. It's the first time she's ever done anything like that. But he doesn't complain or judge; he doesn't care. He spends the morning playing with his son until the mother comes down in the same dress and bonnet she had on the first day he arrived. Cain's confusion is overruled by his determination not to let them leave by themselves like the last father did.

Cain follows the dirt road that he failed to notice this whole time there. Walking on the dirt path, Cain sees a bunch of poorly kept farm fields beyond the tree line. A sign on the side of the dirt road catches Cain's eye.

"Welcome to Elkport, Iowa!"

The town is a small town filled with various shops and businesses. Every person in the town looks just like Cain's family, except their shell-like skin is various colors and shades. It is clear that some celebration is going on in the town. Every building has a wide open door, and the creatures are coming and going as they please. Everyone is doing something. Some are making food, Cain notices that they only cook bacon and other various meats, but only Cain eats. His family simply cuts it up and moves it around their plate and then throw it out later. Other creatures place decorations or run games. The only exception is the church. It is closed, and there doesn't seem to be anyone inside.

Walking up to the church, Cain looks through the windows and sees a man inside curled up in a ball. Another human person, a balding old man in priestly robes. Cain's eyes go wide, and he can't look away from the stranger. The priest, sensing something, opens his eyes from his sleep and makes eye contact with Cain. The two stare at each other. The priest quickly gets up and runs towards the church doors. Cain feels like running, but notices his wife and child are too far away. He can't grab both of them and leave in time before whatever is about to happen happens.

"You, who are you?" the priest asks, getting to Cain faster than Cain could think. "I'm Cain. Who are...Who are you?" Cain stutters.

"Who'd you kill?" the priest asks, his eyes becoming daggers digging into Cain's flesh. Cain's eyes dart to his wife, who is carrying some baskets with other creatures also in various colored dresses. The priest catches the look and follows his eyes before Cain can react. The priest nods.

"Who is she to you?" The priest asks with an intense sense of urgency.

"She's my wife, I can't...."

Cain doesn't know what to say; he doesn't know how to defend himself. His worry and fear of losing what he had earned are too intense for him to handle.

"I'm sorry," The priest says. "I'm Abraham. I've taken the role of the priest in this town.

Just like you, I killed him and took his role."

"What are you, sorry for?" asks Cain. "Are you gonna...."

"No, I'm sorry because it's hatching season," says Abraham.

"Wha...." But before Cain can ask, Abraham stops him.

"Every year, the people of this town are hatched in front of God and are taken away," says Abraham. "Now and then, someone like you will come in, kill someone, and replace that person. Then, when they hatch, they have to leave us behind. It's not easy, but we're not supposed to be here," Abraham's eyes are filled with regret and sadness on Cain's behalf, which bothers Cain. Cain doesn't like Abraham's eyes; he doesn't like the human Abraham is. He doesn't like Abraham's words. Cain can't understand him, and that upsets him.

Cain understands his new family; he loves them, and they love him. They don't judge him for his minor mistakes, and they make it impossible for him to make any mistakes. They are perfect for him. And now this insane man is telling him something crazy that doesn't make sense. Not letting Cain get in a single word to try and push back against this craziness.

"It's gonna be hard for you, but it'll be okay. They'll get replaced. A new family will come, and you can just love those new ones. That's what I've been doing for years. I cry every time they leave, but they always come back to me in some way. They always do. God can't simply stop making humans, can he?"

That final line causes Abraham to stare off into the distance.

Cain's rage starts to boil up again at this insane man and his words. Cain raises his fist, but before he can act upon his nature, a loud chiming noise comes from the top of the church.

"It's time! I'm sorry, my friend, but I can't be out here to watch this. It's too much for me!" Abraham begins to cry at his own words and runs back into the church to escape whatever is about to happen.

CRACK!

Cain quickly turns around and sees a human hand, with an extremely long arm, stretching far past the sky to touch the top of one of the egg people. Their head cracks open. The hand reaches down inside the creature and pulls out a yellow glob covered in that same thick, clear liquid that came out of the father, and pulls the glob up into oblivion. Then, more hands come down from the sky and begin to collect in mass. Cain panics. He runs towards his wife as she extends her arms towards one of the hands. Cain is about to reach her when he notices that his child is even closer to one of the hands. Cain changes directions.

CRACK!

Cain trips on a lifeless husk of one of those creatures. He picks himself back up, and he hears another.

CRACK!

He turns around to see his wife's insides being gently pulled out by the hand of God.

With tears raining from his eyes, he turns to his son. CRACK!

Cain falls to his knees and screams.

"WHY!? WHY DO YOU PUNISH ME SO HARSHLY! PLEASE HAVEN'T I EARNED! AT LEAST TAKE ME WITH THEM!"

Cain cries into the sky. One final hand comes down and gently places itself on his forehead. Then a splitting pain fills Cain.

***

David sits there on his couch in horror at the news.

"This morning, the missing person, Cain Anderson, was found dead after his car was found in a ditch a few weeks ago. According to authorities...."

David shuts off the TV. He knows what happened. They found Cain split open with his insides missing. David looks down at Cain's car keys and wonders to himself. Was this an act of God?

***

About the Author

Growing up in Iowa and with a weird imagination always leads me down some weird paths in storytelling. I'm sure everyone has come up with a pretty weird story idea from time to time; if not, every story they write is one of those. I am no different.

15

VENGANZA'S CURSE

BY PETER BOYLAN

The trail starts at the back of a cul de sac at the end of a road in an old Honolulu neighborhood built on a foothill of the mountain range that divides the island in half.

A red metal gate at the entrance is shaded by Ibizia trees with their wide, palm-shaped branches that hang over the terrain like an umbrella.

Next to it, a white sign scarred by rust cautions hikers that they are walking into a hunting preserve and to be mindful of the native plants and animals.

The trail starts on a black asphalt track lined by ferns, brush, and grey-barked trees with limbs that reach toward the ground. The leaves on the limbs curve toward the earth like long fingernails in the hot and humid summer months. Snake plants, with their green and yellow leaves twisting together, poke out of the brush in spaces, like reptiles fighting for the warmth of the sun.

The trail tracks along the outline of a ridge, going up and down while gaining 1,700 feet for six miles until you reach the mountain summit. When you stop and turn around you look out at where the land stops and the sea meets the sky.

The last seven hundred feet of the climb through the clouds inspired the legend that the ridge line is where souls line up to enter the afterlife.

Since Hawaii became a U.S. territory in 1900, developers unearthed thousands of burial plots in their efforts to turn the scenic mountain into luxury housing developments.

To the side of each ridge, every five hundred to six hundred yards, long, red dirt trails for pig hunters extend to the riverbeds in the valleys where the grazing ungulates hide in the thick bush next to the water. The trees form a green canopy over the valley floor and along the ridges.

This is where Benjamin Venganza was happiest as a child. He was long, and lanky, with thick black hair. He smiled easy and laughed loud. He grew up in a red and white single-story home along winding road not far from the trail.

As a boy he hiked the ridges and fished in the streams at the end of the pig hunters' trails. The ridges were his playground, a place where he could be alone.

One day after he turned 16, Venganza, wearing green shorts and a black shirt, walked past the red gate, onto the asphalt trail and vanished.

He told his parents he was going to fish for prawns and gather guava. The police and the fire fighters and the hunters looked for him for a month. They used dogs, helicopters, and hope. None of it, including the tear-stained pleas of a frantic mother on the evening news, brought Benjamin home.

Venganza was gone. The search had to stop. His parents moved away. The red and white single-story home he grew up in was sold.

Eventually, everyone forgot about the long, lanky boy.

Five years after he disappeared, on the first Saturday in August, a high school junior, Andrew Angst, 16, was working to clear the trail with his school's service club just inside the red gate.

Their teacher, Mat Malum watched over them like a shepherd, occasionally urging his flock to move around the brush.

Malum stood a slender six feet. He had close cropped blonde hair, blue eyes, and the wired muscles of an avid hiker. He wore a green, wide-brimmed jungle hat and glasses that hung on an oval-shaped face with a slit for a mouth.

The three other boys with Andrew were spaced out along the edges of the trail, each with a large black trash bag. They wore thick yellow gloves made of leather and worn by years of use by the school's landscaping company.

They walked along the trail, their faces fixed on the ground, looking for trash or plants that threatened the native flora and fauna.

Mr. Malum gave each student a five-by-seven laminated notecard featuring pictures of plants for the boys to remove. The State Department of Agriculture donated them to the service club years ago.

Every few feet the boys would stop at a plant, pull the cards from their pockets, and try to match the plant at their feet with the pictures. A match would elicit a shout, and a student would disappear into the depths of the brush and the snake plants, emerging later with a handful of plants.

It was a grey day. A light drizzle and intermittent, whipping winds stopped and started the rustling of the trees.

Andrew was tall with straight shoulders and had the build of a boy who had played first base since he was six. He was fiddling with the heavy gloves that guarded his hands from the thorny work when he heard branches start to break above his head.

Andrew peered up. A body hung from a tree branch. It was a boy. The boy wasn't playing. He wasn't hanging by his hands or knees. He dangled, a noose wrapped around his neck.

The boy's green shorts were stained with splattered blood. The pale skin of his forehead was furrowed around a bullet hole that nearly split his skull in two.

The noose rubbed against the wood of the tree, as the boy's weight pulled it down crackling like wood in a fire. The smell of leaves rotting in a compost pile smothered Andrew.

He had only seen dead people on screens as he scrolled through his adolescence. He had nightmares before, but waking up made it easy to explain away as a dream.

Andrew was awake. His mouth went dry.

A chill seeped through him as the body twisted beneath the branch. Everything was muffled, the rapid thud of his heart all he could hear.

Mr. Malum and the other students continued their work clearing the trail. No one saw the body swinging from the tree above them.

Why can't they see it? Why can I see it?

"Let's go Andrew," Malum, ordered, pointing toward another student who was dragging a trash bag.

Andrew didn't move. He couldn't move. A cold lump sat in his throat in the place where the words come from.

What is this?

He stared up at the body. It swayed back and forth as Malum walked right under it. The dead boy's feet, stretched straight toward the ground, nearly nicking the top of Malum's head with each gust of wind.

Andrew tried to focus on the light tapping sound the rain made when it hit his slicker. He felt his heart beating in his ears. His face was hot.

He extended a finger toward the body and stared at Malum.

"Look," he hissed.

Malum and Andrew looked straight up at the same time.

The body was gone. The branch that bent low was now straight and level with the tree line along the trail. There was no noose. No blood. No body.

Just Malum, staring at him.

"Grab a bag and save the forest," Malum told Andrew as he walked away to check on the other students.

Andrew took off his dark blue baseball cap, shook his head and ran his hand through his black hair. He had not been sleeping well.

His screen time was way up that week with video games, group texts, and YouTube fodder filling his brain with images and dopamine that probably had him seeing a dead guy in a tree that no one else could see.

He unscrewed the top of his water bottle and took a long drink. He poured water on his face. He exhaled and returned to the work.

On that day, Malum had the students searching for Clidemia hirta, also known as Koster's Curse. It was named after the coffee farmer blamed for covering an island in Sweden with the fast-growing, invasive bush that took over the native flora.

Koster's Curse flowers are small and white surrounded by dark purple berries that burst easily, spewing their dark juice. The plants quickly form thickets that suffocate and consume native plants, building dense underbrush that makes the dirt around them easy to turn. The leaves and branches are covered with needle-sharp hairs that can break the skin, producing tiny pinpricks of blood.

The dark purple berries from Koster's Curse popped beneath Andrew's brown hiking shoes, the juice staining the tips of his laces that were untied and dragging in the dirt and debris.

Andrew bent down to tie his shoes. As he crouched, he saw a bouquet of the invasive plant's white flowers growing out of a decayed tree limb on the ground. The black veined green leaves smothered the sapling of a mountain apple tree.

Andrew reached into his pocket for the invasive species card Malum gave him. He wanted to be sure that was the plant to pull. He could not find the card. Andrew turned back to the sapling and saw it bending beneath the weight of the Koster's Curse.

He pulled on his yellow gloves and reached to the base of the thicket and leaned backwards with all his weight. The thicket groaned and his forearms strained. The sound of the cracking base of the plant was muffled by the dirt.

Andrew banged the roots against the tree to shake off the mud. In one clump of mud he saw the corner of what looked like a plastic card.

He bent down and pulled it out of the mud. The card was crusted with old dirt, the images beneath the laminate were faded by the elements.

But Andrew could make out enough of each picture. His eyes slowly scanned the images on the card. They were all plants.

Andrew scraped the card against the tree to peel off the last of the mud. At the bottom of the card, in black block lettering read the name, "BENJAMIN VENGANZA."

He shoved the card into a cargo pocket on his shorts and put the uprooted plant into his trash bag. The rain was heavier now. It tore through the treetops, lashing at the leaves.

"Let's wrap it up," Malum shouted above the din of the worsening weather.

Andrew reached behind his head and pulled the nylon hood of his slicker over his baseball cap and picked up his trash bag. The red gate of the trailhead was hardly visible through the rain. His feet sucked mud up from the trail with each step.

When he reached the red gate, Malum was standing there with a white mesh laundry bag. He held it open for the scouts to put their gloves in it. Andrew dropped his gloves into the bag, walked past the gate, and waited by the sidewalk of the cul de sac for his mom to pick him up.

Later that evening Andrew elected to skip the screens before bed.

He put his phone in a dresser drawer on the far side of the rectangular room he shared with his mother's home office. Andrew's mother raised him alone with the help of her parents who lived with them. She ran an accounting business out of the four-bedroom house they all shared.

Andrew often fell asleep to the tapping of his mother's fingers on her keyboard as she finalized work for clients. She did the books for small businesses, law firms, and helped out with Andrew's school as a volunteer auditor.

When she finished, she would stand up from her chair, walk the three feet to the foot of her son's bed and sit down. If Andrew was awake, she would ask about his day, and they would talk in the dark. On clear nights, moonlight filled their space. If he was asleep, Andrew's mother would sit quietly for a moment before kissing him goodnight. She left the door to the room open so the light from the kitchen would spill into his room.

At about 3:30 a.m., Andrew felt the edge of his bed get heavy, where his mother always sat. She had driven straight to a client dinner after dropping him off at home that afternoon. They had not had time for their nightly talk.

Andrew opened his eyes. He could usually see the outlines of his bookshelf, his mom's desk, and the dresser beneath the one window in the room.

Andrew could not see anything but black. Whoever was sitting on his bed didn't have the same gentle warmth of his mother. In fact, it was shivering cold. The smell of rotting plants, musty and damp, choked his nose until his eyes watered.

He sat up straight and looked at the foot of his bed. The dead boy with the noose around his neck stared back at him.

His pupil-less eyes were black as coal, his hair flat against his pale white skin.

He sat cross legged, his glistening black shirt tucked into his green shorts. The noose hung taut from an invisible branch, tight around the boy's neck.

Blood dripped down from the bullet hole in his forehead, dribbling down his nose and off his chin, pooling on Andrew's white sheets.

Andrew tried to scream but he had no breath. He was frozen. The dead boy stared at him. Andrew didn't know how long.

The dead boy slowly reached both hands toward Andrew. The skin was torn away from the tips, and the nails were broken and worn. His death was hard. He struggled and fought before it ended.

The boy lifted his hands into the darkness above their heads and pulled something out of thin air and dropped it on the bed in front of Andrew.

Andrew looked down and saw the notecard on the bed. The name "BENJAMIN VENGANZA" glowed red on the card.

Andrew looked up and the dead boy named Benjamin Venganza was at his bedroom door. Andrew got out of bed, walked across his room, and stood next to the boy.

Venganza pushed the door open to the hallway. The night light in the kitchen was out. The house was black. Andrew could not see anything.

Venganza took two steps into the blackness and stopped to stare at Andrew.

"Follow," boomed a deep voice in Andrew's head. Venganza turned his back to Andrew and disappeared into the darkness.

Andrew closed his eyes, took a breath, and stepped into the hallway.

He opened his eyes. Andrew stood in a basement. The floor was made of smooth, grey concrete that sloped toward a drain in the center of the room.

Two flickering fluorescent bulbs hummed above, bathing the room in a pale, white light.

The walls were painted black. A brown wooden door with a silver deadbolt and a brass knob was located across from where Andrew stood.

Andrew heard a loud thud overhead. Then footsteps, heavy and fast, getting louder as they got closer. Someone was rapidly descending downstairs toward the door in front of Andrew.

A key slid into the deadbolt. Andrew watched it turn and click open. The brass knob rotated clockwise, and the brown door swung open into the room.

It was Mr. Malum dressed in black nylon sweatpants with a matching black hoodie.

Malum turned back to the stairway and took several leaping steps up the stairs. Andrew watched his service club adviser bend over and wrap his hands around a large burlap bag at the top of the steps.

"You didn't want to play with me," Malum told the bag as he struggled to pull it down the stairs. "I gave you money. I gave you rides. I gave you an A!" Malum screamed at the bag.

Malum dragged the bag into the center of the room above the drain. He reached into his pocket and removed a box cutter. Malum bent over the bag and dug the box cutter into the burlap at the top where it was bunched up.

The fabric popped and shredded beneath the blade. Malum dropped the box cutter on the concrete floor. He gripped each side of the bag and tore it open.

Benjamin Venganza's body lay on the concrete floor wearing a black shirt and green shorts. Duct tape covered his eyes and his mouth. His hands and feet were bound by brown rope.

Andrew saw Venganza's chest rise and fall. He was still alive.

Malum muttered to himself and walked out of the room and up the stairs. Andrew stared at Venganza as the boy breathed slowly on the floor. Andrew tried to move, to do something, but his feet were glued to the floor.

The loud footsteps on the stairs returned and Malum reappeared with a noose in his hand. He held it open and slipped it over Venganza's head, pulling it tight around his neck.

Venganza shook and kicked. He flopped on the floor and tried to squirm away from Malum. Malum threw the end of the rope over a bundle of water pipes that ran across the roof of the basement.

Malum took the end of the rope in both hands and dropped his weight to the floor.

Venganza's body flew off the floor and snapped straight. He wiggled like a fish pulled out of the water and suspended from a hook. Andrew heard a crack and Venganza's neck snapped to the right. He stopped moving.

Sitting on the floor, Malum reached into his left pocket and removed a silver .45 caliber semi-automatic handgun.

Malum's face was fixed in a smile. His glasses fogged, his blonde hair matted to the sides of his face. He aimed the pistol at Venganza's forehead and pulled the trigger. Venganza's head snapped back. Blood spattered on the pipe and roof of the basement and poured from a hole in the center of Venganza's forehead.

The gunshot echoed throughout the basement, growing louder and louder in Andrew's ear. He closed his eyes, clasped his hands to the side of his head, shaking it back and forth, trying to force the sound out of his skull.

Andrew got down on his knees and opened his eyes.

He was in his bed. The dead boy was gone. The light from the kitchen slid into his room from the door cracked open to the hallway.

The clock read 5 a.m.

Andrew got out of bed and walked over to his dresser. He pulled on a pair of khaki cargo shorts and a long-sleeved grey hoodie. He grabbed his phone, slid socks onto his feet, and pulled on his running shoes. He walked out into the hallway and headed to the garage door.

Andrew stopped in his garage and bent down to unlock a flashlight from a rectangular charging pod on the floor. He hit the garage door opener. The chain and pulley groaned as the door receded. Rain pounded the pavement of his driveway.

He wasn't sure why he got dressed and where he was going but he was moving. He was being pulled. He had witnessed a murder, however long ago it happened, and now some force had taken control of his body.

Andrew walked out the front door and onto the street. The street was wet and the sky cloudy. It was drizzling. The streetlights were still on, and the patches of sky visible through the clouds were slowly lightening with the coming day.

Andrew walked across the street and onto the sidewalk. He walked past thirteen homes and took a left. He counted each house as he passed it, trying to remember something to get him home from what he had to do.

He found himself at a dead end standing in front of a single-story blue house painted with yellow trim. A mango tree rose out of the backyard, the orange and yellow fruits bouncing beneath the rain drops.

Andrew had never been to this part of his Honolulu neighborhood before.

It started to rain harder. The drops fell fast on the asphalt. Andrew's clothes stuck to his skin, and he felt his socks soak up the rainwater. He looked at the blue house with the yellow trim. Through the rain he saw the dark window of the kitchen through the open-air garage. A light went on.

Andrew saw Mr. Malum walk into his kitchen and fill a coffeepot with water. Andrew felt a cold lump form in his throat. His chest got tight and cold.

"Now," boomed the voice in his head.

Andrew was moving again. His chest was warm and loose. The lump in his throat was gone.

He was soaked through, his clothes hanging like wet rags from his skin as he walked through Malum's garage and stood at his front door.

Andrew stared into the camera of the Ring doorbell for a long moment before reaching up to press the button. He backed away from the door and stared through the lighted window into the kitchen of the home.

Malum turned quickly toward the sound of his Ring. He stood up and walked toward the front door.

Andrew reached into his pocket for his phone. His hand closed around the sharp edges of a five-by-seven notecard laminated in plastic. Malum opened the door.

He stared through the rain at Andrew. "Come in you are soaked," Malum said.

Andrew walked into Malum's house and closed the door behind him. Malum stood before him with his hands at his side. He studied Andrew's face, his blue eyes flickering across his face.

"I'll get you a towel... and some dry clothes," said Malum as he turned to leave the room. "Go ahead and take your clothes off."

"No," said Andrew, forcefully.

Malum stopped and turned back to face Andrew. Andrew reached into his pocket and took out the five-by-seven card with the pictures of the plants on it. He ran his fingers across Benjamin Venganza's name.

He handed the card to Malum who took it and flipped it over in his hand. Malum looked at the name and then back at Andrew.

"I don't know who this is," Malum said, handing the card back to Andrew and taking a step back.

The smell of rotting leaves and mildewed wood filled Andrew's nose.

"Finish," said the loud voice in Andrew's head.

"Benjamin Venganza is right there," Andrew said pointing behind Malum's head.

The teacher turned around and raised his hands to his face, his mouth locked open.

The dead boy Benjamin Venganza hung in the air with the noose wrapped tight around his neck. Blood dripped down his forehead between his black eyes.

He floated close to Malum, his hands flush against his sides.

Venganza's stark black eyes gleamed in the light of the doorway. His pale face cocked left and right, left and right, looking into Malum's face.

His arms flashed forward and he wrapped them around Malum's body, hugging him close.

"I want to play now," the dead boy told Malum, and held him tight.

Malum started to shake. His eyes rolled back into his head. His arms flapped and grabbed at the air. Malum fell to his knees. The dead boy locked his hands behind Malum's back.

Blood poured out of Malum's nose. His neck snapped back. Venganza's mouth opened, and the dead boy screamed.

Andrew slammed his hands on is ears and closed his eyes. Venganza screamed and screamed and screamed. Then he stopped.

Andrew opened his eyes. Malum was dead, his blond hair matted to his skull as it lay in a pool of blood.

Venganza reached out his hand and placed it on Andrew's head.

Andrew sat straight up in bed. He was dry. Sunlight poured through his window into his room. It was a dream. Just a really disturbing dream.

He checked the clock. It was 5 p.m. He'd slept all day.

Andrew dressed and walked into the kitchen. His mother sat reading the evening newspaper, a glass of red wine next to her. She greeted her son and slid his plate of cold toast, eggs, and papaya across the table.

Andrew asked her what she was reading.

"You wouldn't believe it," she said, her eyes never leaving the page. "They found Mr. Malum dead in his house this morning. Pretty gruesome.

"There was a boy's body in his basement," his mother added.

"Benjamin Venganza" said Andrew, a lump returning to his throat.

About the Author

Peter Boylan was born and raised in Honolulu, Hawaii but credits his career as an ink-stained wretch with five years in Iowa City, Iowa, allegedly as an undergraduate English major and one-time Daily Iowan correspondent. Boylan dedicates his days to chronicling crime in Honolulu.

16

DON'T TOUCH JENNY'S THINGS

By Dace Carlisle

While the characters in our stories require motivation to hold readers' attention through, it's the characters in real life whose random acts can cause a cocked-up hullabaloo.

Such was the case of Mikey Bolden, whose outlook on life was never so golden as the time he met the spirited woman to whom he'd become beholden.

No job was too big for Mikey you see. He could handle a lathe, a band saw, and torches of acetylene. He'd fasten the bolts and tamp down the nails for any unionized company.

In Storm Lake or Cherokee, in Adel or Ankeny, Mikey Bolden was as dependable as a train in Germany.

Or Switzerland, depending on your appreciation for geography.

Ol' Mikey Bolden traveled Iowa from town to town providing his services of grit. Building roads, ditches, and storage sheds for the government.

There was no way of knowing that Mikey's last occupational accompaniment would be in Vinton—a country town and one time railroad settlement.

In the summer of '87 Mikey was there tacking shingles to the roof of a county shed with no way of knowing what absurd adventure lay ahead.

Usually on Mikey's temporary jaunts he stayed in local haunts like the motel X or with a cordial friend, but with the boisterous Benton County Fair afoot, Mikey found no room at the inn.

Instead, he found a spot in a clapboard boarding house across the tracks from the old rail depot. Up in the attic there was one room where Mikey could lay low.

Growing up ,Mikey Bolden was from Nowhere. A town between here and there. He didn't care for corn. He had no patience for beans. But Mikey could drive a Firebird like Jeffrey Bodine.

In his youth he prowled construction sites to pilfer tools. Smoked Camel wides outside the Super O and felt up girls from the reformatory school.

When his older brother Ricky returned from boot camp he taught Mikey how to cook ice. They set up shop out in a trailer park called Shady Paradise.

They pocketed cold meds from the pharmacy. They cruised cornfields for anhydrous. They snatched batteries from friends' remote controls so they could cook up some white Christmas.

Out in Shady Paradise the fumes mingled and tingled. The chemistry was electric. Then with his lighter Mikey made it all go boom with one fatal flick.

Mikey was blown clear of the blast. He lost his left eye to shrapnel and suffered a scratch on the ass. All that was left of his brother Ricky was teeth, bone, and ash.

Ricky was buried but there was no money for a headstone. Mikey spent ten years in Anamosa following orders from the warden's megaphone.

His youth was lost. So were his family and home.

In Anamosa, Mikey kicked his habit but even a nun'll take a nip of hooch to keep good form.

So while the Jacks and Cindys of Vinton were in the next town watching fireworks on the Fourth, Mikey was up in his room half a bottle deep wishing he'd never been born.

The room was a squalor of empty tins of chicken pot pie and brown cups of slurpy chew. Mikey nodded as his transistor radio played Alan Walker singing about Chattahoocheecoo.

And Mikey rolled his glass eye in his palm, staring at the locked door on the opposite side of the room. Something was locked away inside Mikey's little bungaloo.

The door had a golden knob Mikey wasn't supposed to touch. In the other room were Jenny's things. Jenny's things were to remain locked. Mikey knew this much.

Don't touch.

Don't touch Jenny's things.

How did Mikey know? Ricky told him. His brother Ricky knew everything.

Ricky followed Mikey from town to town. Looking over little brother's shoulder. Making sure Mikey's secret past was never to be found.

Ricky appeared in Mikey's dreams. His face burnt to a crisp and speaking with a crackly lisp. He warned Mikey of roiling storms, shady deals, and the best places to buy porn.

Since Mikey arrived in Vinton, Ricky's nocturnal visits were as pesky as his jock itch. "Don't touch the golden doorknob," the charred Ricky admonished. "Jenny's a crazy bitch."

"Who's Jenny?" Mikey finally asked one night, tossing and turning in a flop of sweat. "She's a girl," said Ricky's ghost. "Caught in an eternal predicament."

"Why?" asked Mikey. "What did she do?" "It's not what she did," answered Ricky. "It's what was did to her and what she'll do to you."

Then Ricky was gone, and Mikey was awake. He was alone in the attic. The moon still shone for goodness sake and Mikey's imagination was in full jail break.

Was Ricky's warning to be followed? Who was Jenny? Why would she bring Mikey sorrow? He knew one thing—he'd be no good for work tomorrow.

There was a scratch at the door. Not Mikey's door. The other door. Jenny's door. The golden doorknob jiggled. It rattled. Mikey would sleep no more.

He rolled his glass eye in his hand waiting for Jenny to appear. The golden doorknob went still at dawn, and Mikey wallowed alone with his fear.

He went to work later that day pounding shingles on the shed. He hit his thumb with the hammer. He dropped a bucket of round heads. It was enough noise to waken the dead.

"Fer Christ's sake!" hollered his boss. "Get yer ass in gear!" Mikey never felt exhaustion and dizziness so severe.

He sat on his lunch pail to take a break. He drooped his head and closed his eyes. He saw the golden doorknob, and behind it was his prize.

His boss came over to Mikey. He handed him a Skoal tin. Mikey stuck a glob of chew under his lip and was set to work again.

"What's goin' on Mikey?" asked his boss. "Ya feelin' sick?" "Nah," said Mikey, shaking his head. 'But there's somethin' goin' on up in that attic."

Work started up in a hazy cacophony. Mikey's boss, a local boy, yelled over the din, "Oh! You must be talkin' 'bout the ghost of dear ol' Jen."

"What?!" yelled Mikey, cupping his ear. His boss chuckled and his belly rolls shook. Mikey waited for the noise to subside and his boss attached a load of lumber to the crawler crane's hook.

"What?" asked Mikey when it was quiet again. "Who's Jenny?" His boss gummed his chew and spat in a nearby dust bin.

"Jenny," said his boss. "The girl with the golden eye. She lived locked up there in your attic. Her ghost is still alive. Some say she never died."

"The girl with the golden eye?" asked Mikey, tapping the glass eye beneath his own lid. His weary head was a whirligig.

"Just a story," laughed his boss, spatting some more chew. "Now get back to work. We gotta a lotta shit to do."

That night, lying on his stained mattress Mikey slept in fits. Half asleep and half-awake the ghosts came to him in shifts.

All the while the clock went tick, tick, tick.

The golden doorknob turned click, click, click.

Mikey leaned over into his wastebasket and upped his sick.

Ricky knocked first.

It was young Ricky who looked as Mikey liked to remember him. Stringy black hair, a bounce in his step, and heroin thin.

The smell of menthol permeated the room. Having Ricky at his bed-side lifted Mikey from his gloom.

The doorknob stopped its racket. "What's going on?" Mikey asked. "I don't know how much longer I can take it."

Ricky sat cross-legged in a folding chair his cigarette already lit. "Sometimes to be beat a crazy woman," he said. "You gotta go batshit."

"Woman? What woman?" asked Mikey, and the golden doorknob gave a little wag. With a start he looked back at Ricky who calmly took another drag.

"That's just Jenny," said Ricky. "And she's stuck. She's stuck in love. She's in love with love. And she's stuck in a trunk.

"You know what else is in a trunk," Ricky continued. "Gold." Ricky nodded his head and his sly look made Mikey feel more bold.

"There's gold in the room?" asked Mikey. "For sure?" "One hunk of gold," said Ricky. "And it's worth enough to keep you fat and happy til you're gray and old."

"The eye," said Mikey quietly. "Jenny's golden eye." Ricky nodded again. There was treasure to be found, and Mikey was the right guy.

"Seduce her," whispered Ricky. "Make her hot for you. Make her lower her guard and she will lead us to her treasure true."

"But how?" asked Mikey. "I am but a man." "Oh but her passion burns bright," said Ricky. "She falls head over heels for any stallion in her sights."

"That's why she was locked up here. She pestered young Reverend Peter so fervently that he lived in holy fear.

"For her own safety, and for the safety of those she held dear, passion- ate, golden-eye Jenny was locked up in here in where she lived out the rest of her years."

"She died up here?" Mikey asked. Ricky nodded and blew out a stream of smoke. Mikey girded his loins and built up his muster to seduce someone who already croaked.

"What do I do?" he asked. "She'll come to you," said Ricky. "Tonight. She's excited to have a man up here—someone to hold her tight."

Mikey thought of all the women he had loved. They all loved him most for his meth. Maybe his love followed them to their death.

"I will do it," said Mikey. "I can make a woman out of a ghost." Ricky dropped his menthol cigarette on the floor and leaned in close.

His face was now as Mikey last saw it. Charred to the bone with exposed tendons clinging to tissue and his jaw wired shut.

"You owe me," growled Ricky through clenched teeth. "You left me to burn and now I rot far beneath."

The cracked black skin crumbled from Ricky's face like paint chips flaking off the fence at their grandma's century place.

"I burned and now it's your turn," howled Ricky as his body broke apart. The golden doorknob rattled. Mikey's stomach churned. Ricky yelled, "Burn, burn, burn."

Ricky faded away. Menthol smoke cascaded through the air. Mikey waved his hand to clear the room of Ricky's ominous prayer.

The smoke dissipated and the sound of the rattling doorknob faded. How long would it be for Jenny to come? Mikey did not know. So he waited.

First came the smell of jasmine and there she stood. A squat woman at the foot of his squalid bed. Her curly hair wild. Her pearly skin smooth. She was Jenny, the amorous undead.

She wore the farmwife dress of cotton with a frilled collar in shades of charcoal. In place of her left eye was a dark, vacant hole.

Jenny had the vacuous smile of ghosts and placated addicts. She raised her hand and beckoned Mikey to join her there in the attic.

Mikey was compelled to stand at attention in his briefs. He was enraptured with Jenny's ample spirit, yet his mind staggered in disbelief.

Then Jenny opened her mouth wide as if to sing. Instead, words in a husky woman's voice appeared inside Mikey's being, "Don't touch Jenny's things."

Mikey averted his gaze from Jenny's chest and mistakenly looked her in the eye. Jenny raised her brow, and Mikey felt the urge to mount this busty succubi.

"What can I do?" Mikey asked, rolling his glass eye in his hand. The image of a gravestone appeared surrounded by weeping willow and rolling farmland.

A length of chain was wrapped around the gravestone. The chain was clamped shut with a padlock. The name on the grave read, "Genevieve 'Jenny' Hancock.'"

The vision vanished and Mikey asked, "Where is it?" Jenny gave him a mischievous smile and, poof, that was the end of their visit.

Jenny was gone. Mikey was alone. All he could think of was her imprisoned underneath that shackled headstone.

Outside the sun was coming up over the trees. Mikey went to his tiny bathroom to take a pee. On the side of the sink sat one brass key.

Mikey held up the frigid key with skeleton teeth to his good eye. It was time for Mikey to play the good guy.

He threw on his clothes. Jumped in his Firebird, brass key in hand, and peeled out to the tune of his Alan Walker jams.

The key would unlock Jenny's heart. Jenny's heart would lead Mikey to the golden eye. He looked in the rearview mirror for a quick take. Mikey jumped. He slammed on the brakes.

She was there. She was in the rearview mirror. The cab of the car smelled of jasmine, and Jenny's empty eye stared at Mike there in the car's interior.

Mikey whirled around. The cab of his Firebird was empty, but Mikey could feel Jenny's heat. The smell of jasmine subsided, and Mikey took a sharp left on 61st Street.

He followed the country roads taking lefts and rights. There was nothing to keep him company but the cows, corn, and flickering sunlight.

Mikey smelled jasmine again and stopped the Firebird. He leaned out his window and saw a two-wheel road overgrown with weeds and filled with cow turds.

He parked the car and ambled down the muddy tracks. His boots squelched and swarms of mosquitoes attacked.

He dove deeper through the brush. He stumbled into a willow grove. The earth was covered in fine grass. Mikey had found his treasure trove.

A crooked, worn gravestone peeked out from under the tall grass. It was wrapped in a rusty chain. Mikey pulled out the skeleton key and rubbed the worn brass.

As he leaned over the stone the smell of jasmine wafted in the stand. Mikey found the brittle padlock. He lifted it, and it crumbled in his hand.

The chain fell loose to the ground. The sparrows twittered, and from under a willow tree came a rustling sound.

Out from the weeping branches stepped Jenny. A heavenly light surrounded her in a ring. She smiled and from her own lips said, "You may touch Jenny's things."

Mikey and Jenny squirmed together under the willow tree til the setting sun. When they were done Jenny gifted Mikey her hairpin and said, "I must go," and she was gone.

When Mikey arrived home the street lamps of Vinton were the only light. His landlord was outside his house watching as his dog sniffed at a chained-up bike.

"Hello," mumbled Mikey as he passed him. "Evenin'," said the landlord, and he gave the air a sniff. "What's that I smell? Jasmine?"

Mikey stopped. He watched the landlord's dog pee on the bike. "What do you know about that space in the attic?" Mikey asked casually, expecting the landlord to say, "Take a hike."

"What do ya wanna know?" asked the landlord, who was holding a bottle of Olds. "What about that doorknob?" asked Mikey. "Is it really made of gold?"

"Who you been talkin' to?" laughed the landlord. "The ghost?" Then he turned, looked in his open first-floor window and hollered, "Goddammit Marjorie I said I wanted toast!"

From inside the wife let out a whimpering apology. And Mikey said, "Yes. The ghost indeed. What do you know about the ghost named Jenny?"

The landlord's dog snuffed at Mikey's leg. The landlord glared quizzically at Mikey and said, "Don't tell me you fell for that old gag."

Mikey let the comment slide. He waited for the landlord to continue and the landlord finally replied, "Somebody's been taking you for a ride.

"Look," he continued, "I've only owned this house since last fall. It was my grandma's until she fell down the stairs at the Legion Hall.

"Granny did like to tell tall stories though. After a nip of Schnapp's she'd talk about her great auntie so-and-so.

"Said her auntie could do some sorta voodoo. She did this magic trick to make men go head over heels, make them chase after her wet little hoohoo.

"But, like, she was too weird. Went too far. Drove a nail through her eye to stay young forever. Family had enough. Locked her in the attic and there you are. All a bunch a poo poo."

"Huh," said Mikey. "Did she have a golden eye?"

"Hell if I know," said the landlord, watching his dog take another leak. "Just a story. And hey, you gonna pay rent? It was due last week."

"Yeah, yeah," said Mikey shuffling away. He slunk to the side staircase that led to the units upstairs. His head spun. What did that landlord say?

When Mikey reached the attic Jenny was there. She waited by his bed. Mikey kissed her naked eye. They snuggled in bed together. There they stayed night and day letting their love fly.

Elation washed over Mikey in a glaze. He kept his glass eye on the nightstand so he and Jenny could share their eye-to-eye gaze.

He missed work. Overdue letters from the landlord piled up under the door. Then one morning instead of jasmine Mikey was struck with a menthol odor.

Ricky was back. Jenny was gone. Ricky rolled Mikey's glass eye along the floor.

Ricky looked as he had before the explosion. Black nubs instead of teeth. Fingernails all gnarled. Pulsing blisters on his cheeks. "Where's the gold?" Ricky snarled.

Mikey searched the room for Jenny. It was only him, Ricky, and the methylated stench. "Get up!" Ricky shouted, holding Mikey's shirt like a winch.

"You smell like a horny witch," Ricky hissed. Then Ricky was gone. Jenny wasn't there. Mikey was dismissed.

That day he went back to work. His boss gave him a shovel and told him to dig until he ran out of dirt.

As Mikey dug and dug he felt Jenny by his side. When he hit layers of saturated shit her jasmine essence made the stink subside.

When he drove home he saw Jenny's image in the mirrors of his car. She smiled. Mikey smiled. The Firebird's engine purred.

Mikey started brushing his teeth at night. Jenny was there in his bathroom mirror making sure he flossed just right.

In bed there was a constant tap-tap-tap on his head. Wake up. Wake up. Jenny needed her man to keep awake the dead.

When Mikey made it to a construction site, Jenny slashed the hydraulics on his excavator just so he could be with her. With fluid flying everywhere Mikey cursed his new life partner.

Jenny hid Mikey's keys so he couldn't leave. She caressed his glass eye. She listened to him breathe. On the toilet she flipped over the tissue so he had a fresh sheet.

In the shower Jenny wrote love poems in the steam. *I ache for your touch. If you leave me I'll kill you. Ha ha. You are my dream.*

Finally one morning Mikey drove north down Highway Two Eighteen. He looked in the rearview mirror. Jenny was there. Her grimace was mean.

In the bed of the Firebird was a new chain. A new padlock was in the glove box. Mikey was done with this game.

When he turned on 61st Jenny took the wheel. The car swerved. Mikey jerked it back before he got killed. They careened down the road. It was just Mikey and Jenny and love and hate and a whole world of feels.

They went left. They went right. Mikey turned the car south. He floored the gas. He tore the wheel from Jenny's grasp. Then Jenny smooched Mikey like everything was left in the past.

The kiss was smothering, slobbery. But Mikey held the wheel so tight his knuckles ached. He saw the dirt road heading off to Jenny's grave and he slammed on the brakes.

He hustled to the bed of the truck and lifted out the chains. He stumbled through the brush and scurried down the tracks under the strain.

The wind whipped up. The brush slashed at Mikey's thighs. And the words, "Don't touch my things," materialized.

Mikey found the willow glade. There was the gravestone. He knelt to his knees and wrapped the chain. He readied the padlock... and stayed.

He put the locket in his pocket. Jenny whispered in his ear, "Forget about it."

"Forget about it."

They sat together under the willow tree. Mikey stared down his ghostly sweetie. "Where's your golden eye," he asked. "Don't bullshit me."

"At home," said Jenny, meekly. "I'll meet you there. Whatever you do, don't leave me here."

Mikey drove. He looked in the rearview mirror. Jenny was there. He looked in the right mirror. Jenny was there. He looked in the other mirror... Jenny.

When Mikey pulled up to the house his landlord waited at the stairs. There was a police officer with him. Officer Johnny Cares.

"Mike, you can't come through!" gushed the landlord as Mikey barreled home. "Whatever," grumbled Mikey. "What you gonna do?"

Mikey pushed passed the posse without hassle. He bounded up the stairs. He heard pounding steps behind him coming up the tower of Jenny's castle.

Mikey lurched inside his home. He slammed the door. Locked the bolt. There was scuffling outside. Jenny rushed up to Mikey and gave him a jolt.

Mikey dropped the chains and padlock to the floor. He ran his fingers up Jenny's thigh. "Tell me," he cried. "Tell me where's your golden eye."

Mikey's hands went cold. He slapped his knuckles on his knees. From Jenny's fingertips to the depths of heaven and hell the ice coursed through Mikey's veins and incarcerated his blood in a freeze.

"Do you love me?" asked Jenny.

"Huh?" asked Mikey. "Wha... what? What do you want of me?"

"I want you to love me," said Jenny. "Forever and always. I want God to rejoice because there was never a love as strong as that between you and me."

Mikey's hands... arms... body... were icy, stuck like glue.

Yeah," he said. "Me too."

Mikey freed one hand and shakily reached up to Jenny's open eye socket. He reached in the hole, pulled out a sharp hairpin, and dropped it.

Jenny's wild hair was like cotton candy caught in the blades of a windmill. Her hands dropped from Mikey's grip. Her face froze and she lost her will.

"Mikey," she squeaked out of the side of her mouth, her smooth skin now wrinkled. "Say you'll love me. Say you'll love me forever. Say you love me still."

Mikey unthawed. He circled round his rapidly aging girlfriend, enjoying her warbled trills. Was this it? Was this the end of their passionate thrills?

"Where's your golden eye?" asked Mikey, tapping Jenny on her head. Tap. Tap. Tap. Ratta tat. "You know me. I'm good for a chat."

Mikey picked up her crusty hairpin. He looked at the golden knob. Behind that door Mikey had one last job.

"Don't..." uttered Jenny through her frozen lips. "Don't touch my things." Mikey laughed in Jenny's face. He had his spectral lover dangling from puppet strings.

Mikey shoved Jenny, frozen as a statue, down to the floor. He stuck Jenny's hairpin in the keyhole of the door.

"My eye..." wheezed Jenny. "My golden eye. Don't touch... Don't touch my.... Let me show..." Mikey cut her off. "Don't worry my love," he said. "I already know."

Mikey turned the golden doorknob. He cranked it. He twisted. The knob came off in his hand. The golden eye really existed.

The smell of menthol permeated the room and obscured the jasmine odor.

"No," cried Jenny, frozen to the floor. "No, don't do it. Don't do it, mi amor."

Mikey inspected the golden doorknob with his good eye. He turned to look at Jenny. "Sorry babe," he said. "I don't love you no more."

Mikey heard a lighter flick and his glass eyeball rolled across the floor. Flames erupted in the waste bin and the cops were banging on the door.

The glass eye bounced off the wall like it was heading for corner pocket. Mikey looked at the golden doorknob in his hand. He popped it into his empty eye socket.

Jenny wilted into the floorboards. The slutty witch of Vinton was no more.

The banging became louder, and menthol smoke billowed above the bed. Mikey heard Ricky's laughter and his smoker's cough. They did it. This was the end.

Then the brothers laughed together and up in smoke they went. Just brother and brother. Enjoying life and death infinite.

***

About the Author

Dace Carlisle is the pseudonym of Hayseed Press co-founder Nick Narigon. He thinks it sounds cool. While writing and editing all these creepy stories, Nick had a nightmare where he was in a graveyard and there was a gravestone for Jenny that had a padlocked chain wrapped around it. As he woke up he was issued the warning, "Don't touch Jenny's things." Nick decided then and there he needed to write Jenny's story, but for some reason he wrote it in rhyme.

Other titles from Hayseed Press

**A Boy on the Farm
By Joseph E. Narigon**

A memoir of growing up on
a family farm during
Depression Era Iowa.

**The F-Man Himself
By Nick Narigon**

A personal love song to
teenage angst and the '90s
alternative era.

*Find these titles and more at
hayseedpress.com*